The Pisstown Chaos

The Pisstown Chaos

A Novel
by
David Ohle

Soft Skull Press
New York

Part of this novel appeared in Parakeet.

Library of Congress Cataloging-in-Publication Data

Ohle, David.
  The Pisstown chaos / by David Ohle.
     p. cm.
  ISBN-13: 978–0–9796636–7–3 (alk. paper)
  ISBN-10: 0–9796636–7–9 (alk. paper)
  I. Title.

PS3565.H6P57 2008
813'.54—dc22

                                        2006100983

Cover design by Shane Luitjens
Interior design by Anne Horowitz
Printed in the United States of America

Soft Skull Press
New York, NY
www.softskull.com

Hats off to Lucille. A nod to Roger.

"We die that we may die no more."
—Herman Hooker, *American Divine* (d.1857)

One.

Victims of the Pisstown parasite were thought of as dead, but not enough to bury. Gray, haggard, poorly dressed, they lay in gutters, sat rigidly on public benches, floated along canals and drank from rain-filled gutters. City Moon, the Pisstown paper, dubbed them "stinkers." Had you walked through Hooker Park, where groups of them congregated, you would have been wise to hold your breath as long as possible. In the end stage of the parasite's devastation, the body decomposed rapidly, starting with the belly. By then internal organs had begun to dissolve. Had you been sitting next to a fourth-stage stinker, perhaps on a pedal bus, when the parasite finished its work, and you didn't move quickly enough, the poor creature might have spattered cadaverine all over your clothing. And the eye-watering odor would never have washed out, not after a million launderings. Despite these sufferings, complete death for stinkers was long in coming, sometimes taking the better part of a lifetime.

Those in the third stage of the infestation often fall into lives of murder and mayhem. In Pisstown, two of them recently asked Reverend Hooker for a starch bar, and on being refused, set upon him with jackknives, leaving him with a bloodied face and a nicked ear. Then they stopped at the home of Peter Gramlich, a prominent wig, and asked at his back window for crusts, for urpmilk, for a lump of willywhack or an old sock full of urpseed meal, for whatever could be spared. When Gramlich denied them anything, they were on him in a moment, cutting him to death with their knives, burning the wood-frame cottage to a mound of cinder with Gramlich inside.

This week we celebrate Reverend Hooker's sixtieth birthday. Now, more and more facts have come to light about the American Divine: anyone who stepped on his shadow was given what he called a "damned Russian punishment." He had one of his aspirants put to death by garrote because he "looked like a pinhead." He forbade his pedalers to make left-hand turns and called the left-hand seat of the vehicle behind the pedaler "the death seat" and never sat there. He once bought a sparrow dyed yellow from a grifting stinker who told him it was a canary. He liked to turn his eyelids inside-out and look at himself in the mirror. His overstimulated immune system contributed to psoriatic breakouts that showed themselves in pulsing red patches, some the size of playing cards. They occurred on his face, chest, legs, arms, and once or twice on the penis and scrotum. The patches came and went with time. When one vanished in a shower of white flakes, another sprouted somewhere else. Like clouds, they showed a variety of contours. Sometimes the Reverend could see a face in them. He named them and spoke to them in hushed tones. There are those who have reported seeing the Reverend on downtown pedal buses, whiskery, uncommunicative, aphasic, intoxicated, tugging at his hair, foaming at the mouth, in rumpled clothing, unable to remember his name.

The departure of a female imp from one of the Heritage Area's most popular parks has left residents in a state of sadness. For the past five years, the imp had been living beside the brackish waters of a small lagoon in Hooker Park, and its presence inspired a devoted following. It was often spotted swimming along the lagoon's edges, munching grass on its banks. In winter, when the grass was gone, it ate the protein-rich scum, spirulina, which floated in foaming islands on the lagoon six months of the year. The imp dragged the scum ashore with its webbed feet, then patted it into little biscuits and let them dry in the sun.

Last month, in a daylong journey, the imp swam across the lagoon, down a canal, and into the Bum Bay Straits. The Reverend's Divine Guard, fearful the animal would wander into ship traffic or be drawn away in an undertow, made a successful effort to net her from a barge. Fearful she could wander again into harm's way, the Guard resolved not to return her to the lagoon, releasing her instead on the Reverend's Square Island Research and Development Farm. "She's a perfect specimen," said Hooker, who had glimpsed the imp twice at the lagoon. "She must be saved for research and development."

In keeping with the Reverend's expressed wish, the prison facility on Permanganate Island will soon stand aside as the Island's primary feature. Now, a complex of buildings has been constructed near the Island's eastern shore, far from the prison itself, devoted entirely to parasite eradication research. A group of the Reverend's researchers has declared its intention to live on the Island and to study the mysterious parasite until the puzzle of its life cycle is solved.

An incident that took place more than a year ago was reported in today's City Moon. At 12:30 in the morning two Pisstown residents were pedaling down Dunvant

3

Road when the paving stones collapsed beneath them into a pit nearly thirty feet deep. As they struggled to climb out of the subsidence, the two were asphyxiated by a mixture of carbolic and cadaverine gases rising from the disturbed ground. After the vapors had dissipated, curious townfolk began digging deeper, looking for the source of the horrific odor escaping the hole. In all, seventeen stinkers were found and, from them, over five hundred teeth extracted, yielding a hefty half-pound of tooth gold.

The stinkers were stacked in a field near the edge of the City. It was supposed that in time, wind, sun, rain and vermin would turn them into dust. But a night watchman at the Palace Orienta, passing the field on his way to work, saw imps feeding on the remains and became alarmed. When he went to the Guard office and reported what he had seen, he was informed that others had filed similar reports, of imps favoring flesh over grass. The Guards had no explanation for the sudden change in feeding habits.

When the first shifting programs were enacted decades earlier, Mildred Balls, known then as Mildred Vink, was a young woman of twenty-five. Hundreds of thousands of shiftees were on the move in those days, headed for new mates, jobs and living quarters. Shifting orders arrived in the mail without forewarning and relocation assignments had to be carried out within days, sometimes hours.

One of those in transition at the time, Jacob Balls, had made a living selling Jake powder in cities, settlements and bailiwicks until he was shifted to the waiting camp at Witchy Toe. He had a light-bodied, fast moving pedal coupe and had called on customers over a wide territory. The finely-grained, yellow-tinged powder was of his own invention. In the trunk were gallon tins of it. The powder, when stirred into water or urpmilk, produced an intoxicating beverage. Thus far all his patent and subvention applications had been denied, but he was confident of one day seeing Jake in every tavern, restaurant and home.

Mildred Vink stood on the roadside in the hot sun as Jacob's coupe came into view. She raised the leg of her rags to the knee, a common way for hitchhikers to advertise their pedaling potential. While she was generally slender in body, her calf muscles were crisply defined and heavily developed. There were two sets of pedals in the coupe, and two pairs of strong legs made traveling at a good clip that much easier.

Jacob glided to a stop. "Where you headed?"

"The waiting camp at Witchy Toe. I've been shifted."

"Put your bag in the trunk. I'm going to the camp, too. That's quite a set of legs you have. They could support a piano."

Mildred opened the trunk, placed her small bag between boxes of Jake powder, and stepped up into the passenger seat.

"Can you imagine," she said, "they're sending me to live in a trailer and mate with a man I've never met." She patted a circle of sun blisters on her throat with a medicated sachet and strapped her feet into the passenger's pedals.

Jacob shook his head. "The Reverend says the whole process is gender neutral, age neutral, all completely random pairing. It's exciting in a way. Things got so dull after that first big chaos."

Mildred began to pedal.

"Slowly at first," Jacob cautioned. "I'm worried about the chain. Let's pedal in reverse a few turns. Unwind the starter spring a little. Then go forward with a light touch. She's a moody machine."

Their conversation continued as the car sprang forward, then slowed to a steady pace.

"It's all been tried before," Mildred said. "The shiftings."

"Has it, now?"

"By Michael Ratt, one of the last presidents."

"I don't remember him."

"The eightieth. Came right after Dorothy Peters. Don't you know any history? He was assassinated by his enemies. They exploded his campaign balloon. He was right under it."

"Sorry, the only things I really read are the Reverend's writings. What came before them doesn't matter."

"The Reverend is utterly jackbatty. I'm not a Hookerite. Never will be."

"He assumed power fairly and squarely," Jacob said. "I'm all for him now, and proudly so. You won't see me complaining. Look, in any culture, when boredom and apathy take hold, the currency is debased and the decline is irreversible. Within the period of peace and prosperity that follows a Chaos lie the seeds of the next Chaos. The Reverend says that all the time. What could be more of a tonic than a random redistribution of the populace? It's fundamental. Hooker *has* learned a few things from history."

"The whole scheme is idiotic."

"I hear the camp isn't all that bad. The trailers are fairly modern. The food is free, and luckily so is the willywhack. One taste of willy and you must have more, they tell me. It makes camp life and all that waiting more tolerable, they say."

"It leaves me feeling too stiff, half dead, like a stinker. I don't like it. I won't take it."

"You *will* take it. It's compulsory."

"We'll see about *that.*"

As Jacob shifted into higher gears, Mildred focused on the pedaling. "Well, then, tell me, what did you do before all the shifting started?"

"I traveled, sold my powder. It's called Jake, a secret formula. You mix a drink out of it that makes you feel a little happy."

"How interesting," Mildred said. "Isn't it exciting, that so many of us are inventing things these days? What we really need is a faster, lighter machine for getting around in. It could have four sets of pedals. You'd have a triangular frame made of light metal tubing with sets of pedals at the corners and one more at the center of the base. In the middle of the triangle I envision a taut canvas, like a trampoline. As the 'quadraped' speeds forward, with air rushing beneath it, a lift is achieved. The pedaling is easier. Even with only two pedaling, it should go at a brisk pace."

"You seem very smart. And I like the way you look," Jacob said, leaning toward Mildred's shoulder and sniffing her. "No odor at all. Nice. I like that. Listen, I'm looking for a viable mate. I want two children, a boy and a girl."

Mildred thought it over for a moment. "As far as children go, I wouldn't be a good mother. I'm too distracted by my work."

"They won't be mothered, or fathered. They'll be raised more or less as house servants. I'm a free-thinker, dear. And in a few years I'll be rich. I'll have thousands. Everyone will be drinking Jake."

Suddenly, Mildred was convulsed with a sneezing fit. "There's something in the air around here." She raised her chin. The sun blisters had grown into patches of small, fluid-filled pustules scattered over most of her throat and neck in circular configurations. "It isn't the sun doing this. There's an irritant in the air, something caustic."

"I don't smell a thing," Jacob said. "I do know the camp is administered by Hooker's Guards and is on the Reverend's approval list. It should be reasonably sanitary."

"When we get there, I'm supposed to meet my new mate at the local Impeteria."

"Now there's a coincidence. So am I." Jacob angled onto a wide, dirt road.

A pearly pink powder sifted into the coupe and formed dunes on the dashboard. "That dust," Mildred said. "It isn't normal. Look at the color of it."

Jacob wet his finger, touched it to the dust, then tasted it. "Sandy, a little salty. It's just road dust."

"No, it's the residue from something incinerated. Don't you smell it?"

7

"That's quite a nose you have. As I said, I smell nothing but the scented oil on my mustache."

"There must be a stinker crematory somewhere close."

"You have an excitable imagination, and that makes me want you to bear my children even more."

The Impeteria appeared around a hairpin turn. "There it is," Mildred said. She unstrapped her feet from the pedals and got out. "I'll give your proposal some thought. We'll find one another in the camp. How big could it be?" She retrieved her bag from the trunk.

Jacob unstrapped and got out. "Take a tin or two of Jake powder. My compliments."

"Thank you. I'll try it."

"Just mix it with eight parts water, or urpmilk, and two parts powder. If you're a slow drinker, you might have to give it a stir every once in a while if it gets too cloudy."

"I'll remember that." She put two tins in her bag and they entered the Impeteria. A frycook sat alone in a far-back booth, his bloated face deeply inflamed and toadlike. The eyelids drooped and the cheeks sagged pitiably. One of the dim eyes drifted from its focal point, making his gaze disturbing and irritating. His chafed brown shoes and dirty rags were equally unattractive. "Well, now, you two look like a good pair. Hardly ever see that anymore. Yesterday come a six-year-old boy and his baby sister. Whatever that Reverend's plan is, it's way beyond my earthly understanding." His face reddened further, his cheeks puffed out and one jagged tooth sat like a kernel of corn on his lip.

"I'm meeting a Jacob Balls, out of Bum Bay."

Jacob did a little dance. "How perfect! Then you're Mildred Vink."

"I am. I guess we're mates." Of all the possibilities, Mildred considered herself fortunate.

"Okay, Mildred, before we order us some stew, I want to make one thing clear to you. You're young, you're fine, in your prime, and I can't wait to mate." He leaned across the table. "Nice lips. Let me have a taste. Give me a kiss. It's the law, you know. Compulsory mating."

"Perhaps, but not compulsory kissing." She held a checkered gingham napkin over her mouth. "It's too intimate. As far as mating goes, I only ask that you take the slow approach."

She angled forward to sample Jacob's odor. "You don't smell good. This will take time to get used to. Don't hurry me."

"All right, I'll try to be nice and gentle. We'll just talk awhile. You like Hooker's shifting programs? *I* sure do. You should have seen me a month ago. A mate that was three-fourths stinker, six bad, mixed-breed children, three of them step, and an all-night job polishing marble in the Bum Bay Templex. Now look what I got. I'm a happy man. This is a well-deserved upshift."

Mildred ordered the stew.

"We're out," the frycook said. "And I've done warshed the pot. Alls we got is sea slug, pickled."

"Slug's not bad. I'll have an order," Jacob said.

"Just a starch bar for me," Mildred said.

"Something to drink? We got root water that I make myself. It's got gas in it. It bubbles. And we got urpmilk."

Jacob ordered urpmilk, Mildred the root water. When the frycook returned quickly with the food and drinks, Mildred asked, "What do we do now? What's the routine here? How far is the camp gate?"

"After you eat, you catch a pedal bus up to the welcome station. They'll tell you what to do from there."

"I have a car outside."

"Leave it where it is. They'll come and get it. When your wait's over, you'll get it back. You'll have another one in the camp. They're all painted yellow."

Mildred's root water was bitter, but thirst-quenching. She ate her starch bar in silence and watched Jacob place chunks of sea slug along the rim of his plate, then one by one eat them, chewing thoroughly before swallowing. "You've got to chew them exactly a hundred times or they'll rot your kidneys." Each chunk was followed by a gulp of urpmilk. "Hey, pretty thing," Jacob said when the last of his sea slug had been chewed and swallowed, and laid his heavy hand on Mildred's shoulder. "We'll get along just ducky. I know it."

When a camp-bound pedal bus stopped outside, Mildred, Jacob, and six or seven other shiftees climbed aboard. A young American male sitting behind Jacob tapped him on the shoulder. "Hey, look here. See my new bride? She's fifty years older than me and way too stiff. If I'm lucky she'll go to the crematory pretty quick."

Mildred turned to see a one-eyed stinker she guessed to be eighty or older, sound asleep, her dentures protruding. "You'd think they would do a better job of pairing people," the American said.

"They're not even trying to," Jacob said. "That's the whole idea. 'It's all random, completely random, and absolutely necessary.' I'm quoting Hooker when I say that."

Passengers were let off at a barn-like, windowless, rusted-metal Quonset hut. "This is where they check us in and check us out," the young American's aged companion said. "I've been here a lot of times." Her walk was hobbled and she struggled to keep her balance. Mildred took her by the elbow and helped her into the sweltering building through tall, sliding doors, seized by rust in their tracks.

To one side of the cavernous building were hastily and carelessly framed check-in booths, each curtained with burlap sacks sewn end to end. When a booth became empty, the next shiftee in line went in. Forms were there to be filled out and dropped through a slot, small jars to be filled with urine, labeled, sealed and dropped into another slot. When these tasks were completed, registrants were instructed to see one of the several white-smocked nurses who were sitting at small tables doing anal swipes on the other side of the building.

Again, Mildred did what she could to help the stinker along. "I sure hope you don't get it as bad as I got it, lady," the stinker said. "You seem to be nice."

When Jacob's turn came, the nurse said, "Stand behind that screen and lower your rags and briefs. We're looking at anal discharges, to get a baseline parasite count. This is the second phase of the new shift. Word came down yesterday from the Reverend's office. I guess they're doing a study. It's for the public good."

Jacob lowered his pants and pulled down his shorts. He felt the cool sting of alcohol being applied with a cotton swab, then the insertion and twisting of something dull and wooden. "Ouch!"

The nurse withdrew the broken probe. "These probes are not well made. Looks like a little piece stayed in there. Oh, well. Nothing we can do. It won't harm you. Natural processes will dissolve it. Move on, now. Go out the back entrance. You and your new partner will be issued a trailer number, a map, and a pedal car. It's up to you to locate your trailer."

"How large is the camp?" Jacob asked the nurse.

"It would take a full day to pedal around it. So don't get lost. There are Guards at the gate and they'll point you in the right direction. They'll also have you take a strong dose of willy."

New arrivals waited behind the Quonset hut to be issued pedal cars. Camp trustees pedaled them up to the crowd one at a time from a garage so far from the welcome station, it took the better part of an hour. The process was agonizingly slow.

11

At some distance, Mildred saw the young American and his old shift-partner get into their pedal car. Other shiftees knew the half-dead stinker wouldn't be pedaling at all and some of the larger, heavier males got behind the car and gave it a push. It rolled slowly down a slight incline, then gained momentum.

"I'm going to refuse the willy," Mildred said. "What can they do if you refuse? Turn you around and send you home?"

"What's wrong with willy? I hear it's relaxing. And I could use something to ease the pain down there. She left a splinter in my bung, from the probe. It hurts."

"It doesn't surprise me. The swabs were dirty. They used them over and over. Tell me, who owns the patent on the swabs and the probes? Who owns the plant where they make them?"

"The Reverend, I guess."

"Of course."

"So what? He's a good man. He's looking out for us. He's got a plan. I'm taking the willy. It's harmless. That's what they say. It's natural. It comes from urpflanz, a juice from the root. Hooker says it's the perfect plant. It has a thousand uses."

"And I'm sure one of them is to make what's intolerable more or less agreeable."

"You're crazy, girl. You're gonna get into trouble."

A reconditioned pedal car was eventually brought to them, freshly painted bright yellow, but with a dry, rusty chain, grinding gears and a broken windshield.

"We're gonna be a hell of a mating pair," Jacob said, strapping his feet into the pedals, then squeezing Mildred's shoulder. "But I'll take it slow."

At the gate was a small, octagonal guardhouse. Two Divine Guards armed with billy bats played pinochle inside and smoked hand-rolled urpflanz cigarettes. One of them got up languidly and strode to the pedal car with two doses of willy in waxed paper envelopes, a packet of documents, and a bottle of water. "Here's your trailer number, a map to find it, a list of do's and don'ts, and your willywhack." He handed the documents to Mildred and the willy to Jacob. "One for you and one for the woman. Have a swig of water if you like."

"I'm not taking that," Mildred said matter-of-factly. "It doesn't agree with me. I'll take my chances without it."

"I'll take it," Jacob said. "I'll take hers, too, if it's all right."

The second Guard swaggered from the guardpost with his billy bat drawn. "What have we got here, a refuser? Nixing the willy, are you? Get out of the car, both of you."

"It was her," Jacob said. "Hell, I'll take it gladly . . . . Come on, Mildred, take it, please."

"No, I'm not. If it's free, and from the Reverend, it's to be avoided."

"Listen to me, lady. This is willy-10, far, far purer than anything they've come up with yet. Willy-1 was rough, untested, yes, and it killed a lot. But we're nine levels beyond that. Now it's also an anti-parasitic."

"I don't believe it," Mildred insisted.

"All right. That's it. I'm going to shove it down your throat. Then you'll know what you're missing."

Mildred tried to keep her mouth closed and her teeth clenched, but the two Guards overpowered her, brought her to the ground and pried open her mouth. She had no option but to swallow the willy, encased in a gelatin capsule. If she hadn't she would have gagged. After this, Jacob swallowed his dose with a gulp of chalky, off-tasting water.

One of the Guards said, "Okay, get in the car and follow the map. Go north fifty trailers then dogleg east. You're in living unit 8080802. You can find all the things you need either in the unit itself or on the grounds. There are plenty

13

of imps living in the greenbelt that surrounds the camp. Trap them or club them for food. In the camp, you'll have to rely a lot on your own devices." He backed away from the pedal car. "What about willy?" Jacob asked. "How do we get more willy?"

"A wagon comes by once or twice a week, possibly tomorrow, I think. You'll be supplied with willy and commodities, too. Water, starch bars, urpmeal, the works. And don't forget, that dose of willy you just had'll put you to sleep right at curfew. It's time-release, so be warned."

The other Guard leaned into the window. "On your way, now, folks. The sun's going down. Things can get hincty in there at night when the stinkers get restless and roam."

Feeling a surge of energy from the willy, Mildred and Jacob pedaled effortlessly. The car's wheels spun in the dirt as it rolled on at a fast rate and headed up the only hill in the camp.

"This willy isn't bad," Mildred said.

"See, I told you."

"They've improved it a lot."

"It gives me ideas," Jacob said, "I'll trap imps. We'll eat the meat and make hats from the fur. We can sell those and turn a few bucks." He glanced out the window once the hill had been topped and they were gliding down.

Mildred watched a nighthawk streak across the face of the moon, dipping and turning in pursuit of mayflies. "It's a beautiful night. My blisters don't itch any more, and I love the way the moonlight dances over the trailer roofs."

"I feel alive. Full of hope," Jacob burbled.

"Same here," Mildred said. "Resisting it wasn't worth the trouble."

After three or four wrong turns, they located trailer 8080802, which was set far apart from the others at the very edge of the camp, standing against a perimeter fence made of concrete and steel and topped with broken glass. The trailer had been lifted onto concrete piers that were out of level, so that it leaned downward in one rear corner. The few trees that survived in the area were in decline, their foliage tinged with a dry, brown fungus.

A few feet away from the trailer, bees and flies swarmed around a small metal privy, entering and leaving through a vent in the roof. Beside the privy, covered with a canvas tarp were sacks of lime and a small shovel.

"I'm surprised we have no neighbors," Mildred said. "You can't see any other trailers from here." She walked around 8080802, noting the broken jalousie windows and the tattered curtains behind them. She picked up a stick and knocked down a few of the mud-dauber nests that were plastered on the shady underside of the back window awning. The steel drum mounted on the roof to catch rainwater worried her. It dripped from several small rust holes.

Jacob got on his knees and pulled a crate of gel cans from under the trailer. "Okay, we got a shitter, we got lime, we got water up there on the roof, and we got enough gel to last awhile. So far, so good." He entered the trailer to have a look.

Mildred stood near an open jalousie. "How is it in there?"

"It's hot as blazes and it stinks."

The mattress in the bedroom was speckled with yellow mold and sagged under a mat of hair. "Looks like imps been living in here," he shouted.

A jar of dried urpflanz graced the top of a bedside table. A drawer was full of candles and matches. The pellet stove had seen long-term use and was in considerable disrepair. "I can fix that," Jacob said, "but there's no pellets around. We're gonna freeze come winter."

Mildred entered the trailer warily, her hands in the air, careful not to touch any of the dusty, oily surfaces all around her. Something was spattered above the sink, an old stain, years old. It was dark red, almost black, and could have been blood.

Jacob took her hands. "How's about a little smack, honey? Right on the kisser."

"No, not yet. No mating yet. It's almost curfew anyway."

Shortly before ten, when a merciful breeze swept hot air out of the trailer and made it habitable for the night, Mildred and Jacob fell into effortless, willy-deep sleep on the dirty mattress.

Two.

The well-known Doolittle girl has made the news again. Her mother recently attested that the child's progress was not typical. In her first year the deep-set eyes grew dark and animal-like, and she was never known to sleep or cry. Whenever she opened her mouth and let her tongue slither forth, she was fed starch bars. During the long summer days she lay quietly cool in her basement room, staring restfully at a radiating water stain on the pulp-board ceiling. At intervals this state of semi-awareness would lapse, her head would turn into her sour pillow, and a white foam would spill from her open mouth and rapidly harden as it ran down her throat and onto her quilt.

One sultry, wet night, Daisy Doolittle came up from the basement, stood there briefly, said something inaudible to her mother, and left the house. She took a pedal bus to Pisstown, rented a room in a downtown guest house, and placed an ad in the evening edition of the City Moon *seeking a suitable mate.*

The American ship, Amber Princess, *collided with a barge delivering stinkers to the waiting camp at Indian Apple. As a result of this collision, three hundred and ninety stinkers were thrown into the icy Bum Bay Straits. The Reverend's Guards were not informed and therefore took no action. Ten days after the incident, a storm swept through the Straits, scattering the floating stinkers widely.*

Because of clockwise currents in those waters, some of them washed up on the shores of Square Island. Water-logged and slightly frozen, they were taken to the Templex and given strong doses of willy. Soon they were put to hard labor in the Reverend's mining operation there.

The Reverend's brother, Wallace, barged into the Office of Patents and Subventions, bringing something smelly in the sleeve of a newspaper, which turned out to be a pickled imp's foot on the end of a stick. He said the device was designed for use in determining the best plank-spacing in the floor of an imp cage and that he was exploring the notion of raising anemic imps for use in parasite research. Further inquiries were discouraged and the patent denied.

The Home Guard reports that a houseboat was found grounded in the National Canal, which has been at low water lately. There were no lights on its deck, nor any outward signs of habitation. It was a practical box cottage, nicely finished, built atop a barge. The shiplap siding was newly painted and the windows caulked. A plaque above the entry door read, "Pisstown or Bust."

When Guards jimmied the door and went into the parlor, a grisly sight awaited them. It was a family of last-stage stinkers, all burst open at the abdomen. The father reclined in a natural attitude on the davenport, the mother sat erect in a wingback chair, an infant lay on the floor in a sea of rags. The Guards report that parasites covered almost every surface in the room. There were so many on the davenport, it seemed alive.

On entering the parasite facility at Permanganate Island, those in the first stage of infestation were segregated from other prisoners and taken by pedal bus to a staging area where, in the stifling heat of a metal Quonset hut, an older Mildred Vink, now Mildred Balls, and a few other victims were checked in. Diagnostic specimens of stool, blood, urine, semen, and hair were taken, and questions asked. "What is the name and address of the last person with whom you've made lip-to-lip contact, and when did that occur?"

"My late husband, Jacob," Mildred said, "about two or three years ago, as many as five. I don't remember."

"Jacob Balls, the brewmeister?" asked an Administration official who overheard her answer. "Didn't he invent Jake powder?"

"Yes, that's true. Before we met."

"I hated the way it tasted in the beginning, in the early days, and the way it smelled, too. I had to hold my nose when I drank it."

"A few batches were bad. There were manpower shortages during the last Chaos. Mistakes were made."

"Well, Mrs. Balls, here's hoping we can lick your parasites before you stiffen up. They tell me the stiffening feels like you've got one foot in the grave and one foot out. But I guess the Reverend said it best when he said, 'We die that we may die no more.' Once you're over it, you don't have to go through it again."

"Brilliant," Mildred said, and the official moved on.

The questions resumed: "Have you committed to memory the Reverend's *Field Guide to the Satisfied Life*?"

"No. I'm not a Hookerite."

"What are you, then?"

"Utilitarian, I suppose. What's good for the most is best for all."

The clerk shook her head and stamped one of Mildred's forms. "I'm going to put you down as Hookerite anyway. Things will go better for you."

"I appreciate that."

"Now, just in case it comes to it, do you want to be buried or burned?"

"Burned, thank you."

"And the ashes sent to?"

"To my granddaughter, Ophelia. The address is there."

"Yes, I see it. Oh, that's a posh area. Wish I lived there."

"Beware of envy, young woman. It's a green-eyed monster, certain to turn on you."

"All right, I've heard enough of your blather. Take your papers and go to the oath-swearing booth."

Mildred removed her spectacles and wiped the lenses with the sleeve of her rags. "An oath to what?"

"It's on the wall in there. Just recite it, sign the form, and get on with your treatment."

In the oath-swearing line, Mildred conferred with several others about the nature of the oath. One of them had known someone who was treated at the facility. "They said it's foolish not to sign it. You don't want curtailed treatment, do you?"

"That's why they make you recite it aloud. People weren't reading it. They were just signing it. So now there's somebody behind a curtain in there listening. If you don't recite it, you're on a list."

Another piped up. "Have you memorized the Hundred and One Sayings, from the *Field Guide*?"

"I haven't."

"Take our word for it," they said. "It would be the smart thing to do. I'm up to fifty-five myself."

"The Reverend says when you can recite them all from memory, you're guaranteed an upshift next go-round."

"If I don't, if I fail to, what happens to me?"

"Some have been pushed out the back door of the Templex with a hand or a foot missing. Maybe it's a rumor. I don't really know."

"You could be tested any time, stopped by a Guard or an Administrator or a certified wig and told to recite the Sayings."

"Thank you for the warning."

"Remember the first one at least—'We die that we may die no more.'"

"I'll remember that. It's easy enough."

"Yes, but what does it mean? What if a Guard asks you that?"

"I suppose it means that death, being what it is, puts an end to the dying process, which may be worse than death. Or, it could suggest the existence of an eternal afterlife, when one never dies again."

"Those are good enough answers to fool a Guard, who are dumb as dirt. Only the Reverend knows the real, true meaning anyway."

When all the preliminaries were over, someone in a mud-colored Administration uniform stepped up to an outdoor dais and made introductory remarks: "For better or worse, welcome to the Island parasite facility. It should be understandable that we see the need to isolate those with early infestations from the populace at large. We'd have a Chaos that could get out of control, spread like a prairie fire, move slowly for a while, then flare up whenever it finds flammable material. And where do we find the equivalent of such flammable material in our cities, towns and bailiwicks? Does anyone know? It's one of the Reverend's Sayings, number seventy-seven to be exact."

A zealous Hookerite raised her hand. "'We grow to hate things we fear'?"

"Yes. Very good. Now, each of you will be assigned living quarters at some distance from your neighbor. Isolation is the best safeguard until we understand what these parasites really are, and how to bring them under control. All of you are listed as first-stage, so let's hope we have a breakthrough before you advance any further."

After a three-hour pedal bus ride, Mildred was dropped off at her living quarters, an old clapboard shack resting atop four pitted, rust-caked steel pilings, one of which had buckled at a weak point, tipping the shack slightly downward, and many of the steps leading up to the flimsy wooden deck surrounding it had rotted away long ago. The structure looked as if it had been a pre-Chaos watchtower, useful when the land was heavily wooded and subject to fires.

Already fatigued by hours of relentless pedaling, having to heave her heavy baggage and bulk over the empty stairway spaces—and skinning her ankles many times—was almost more than Mildred could endure. She removed her spectacles and lay on the deck all that night, too weak to stand on her feet. When she awoke, a string of saliva stretched from the corner of her lip to the plank beneath her head. With her eyes at floor level, she detected a sudden movement, something small and dark streaking across the deck. Without her spectacles, the bug was too blurred to identify.

In a kitchen cabinet she found a two-month supply of starch bars, a kilo of urpmeal, some ground nuts, a tin of Jake powder and a packet of dried imp meat. On the counter was a five-gallon drum labeled "Safe Drinking Water. Boil First," a case of gel cans and a box of Sur-strike matches. In a drawer were a few cooking utensils, a skillet and a mismatched collection of dinnerware. A wooden box nailed to the wall was full of stationery, pencils, and official Permanganate Parasite Facility stamps.

In the sleeping area, defined by a blanket hanging from a rope, was an acceptably comfortable cot. A few feet away, a commode, dotted with old excrement, signaled that the place had not been occupied for at least a few months. Beside it was a pump handle for drawing water up for the commode and the sink from a shallow well below the tower. A pellet stove sat in a corner next to a crock filled with pellets. On a plastic-laminate table were stacked three boxes of specimen jars and supplies of methyl alcohol and tongue depressors.

In addition to a copy of the Reverend's *Field Guide*, there were items of clothing in an old chiffonier, mostly rags left behind by previous occupants. When Mildred opened the door, she found pinned to it a drawing of a brown spider with the clear marking of a fiddle on its back. She put on her spectacles and read the caption: *"Danger! Loxosceles reclusa - The brown recluse, or fiddleback spider is capable of inflicting a serious bite which may ulcerate and require removal of infected tissue. The species is common in outbuildings, under boards, in attics and other little-used, dry areas, such as this dwelling."*

"Oh, dear," she said aloud, looking at the dusty floor and feeling on her face a steady, warm, dry, late-July breeze. She wondered if the Administration might be able to provide a dust or a spray that would kill them. Meanwhile, she half-filled four specimen jars with water and placed the cot's legs in them, hoping that would keep the spiders away when she was asleep.

A pedal van from the Administration, she had been told, would deliver food and mail on a monthly schedule, and the driver would collect stool samples for analysis. She was to use a tongue depressor to remove a sample from her stool and deposit it in one of the jars, which were to be labeled as to date and time and filled with alcohol.

She had not been allowed to bring any books or other reading material into the facility and her knitting was taken away at the staging area. So, to pass the time on her first full day in the tower, Mildred studied the *Field Guide*'s Hundred and One Sayings for a while, then wrote letters to her grandchildren, knowing it would be months before they got them.

Dear Roe,
    I'm so lonely I could cry. I have nothing to do and barely enough supplies even for that. So I'm writing to my darlings to pass the time. Is your sister taking decent care of you? Are you playing your saw every

day? Please write me in copious detail. Ask your sister for help holding the pencil if necessary. I know how your hands tremble since your grandfather's terrible fall. I'm so sorry you children had to see that.

But I must tell you, I don't know how long I'll be away. And if the parasites get the best of me, I may return in a small box. The fully dead are cremated here and the ashes sent to next of kin by mail. But you know me, I've got plenty of parasite-fighting mental resources to work with. I'm sure I'll come up with something before the little beasts get into my heart.

Love, Grandmother

Dear Ophelia,

They've sent me out to live in the middle of nowhere. There's not much to see. The view from my window is a dry creek bed snaking through a cluster of dead sycamores, scattered palmettos, creosote bushes, wild poppies and urpflanz.

I don't have the creature comforts I'm used to, but it isn't so bad. Though the summer heat is extremely oppressive during the day, a cooling breeze blows at night. There's a pellet stove to keep me warm this winter and a crock full of pellets.

Today was a dreary, hot Tuesday, not a drop of rain or a cloud all day. I found a drowned blackfly at the bottom of my teacup this morning and a few parasites in the stool sample. I don't know how they live on it. Perhaps they don't. Perhaps it's just their mode of transport into this sweet, airy world of ours. Even though my load of parasites is light, I feel heavy all the time, and sleepy.

Watch out for that dreamy brother of yours. You know how his mind can drift. Remind him to check himself for worms twice a day. Make sure he oils his saw and waxes the bow strings. And we don't want him wandering off and getting lost, so make sure he has plenty of ribbons in his pocket when he goes for a walk. He can tie them to bushes and find his way back. And I want you to stay close to home and shave him when he gets his tremors. We don't want him nearly beheading himself again. And don't lock him in the closet when he's being crabby. It gets him excited and he masturbates.

It must be springtime there. Have the hydrangea begun to bloom? What about the wasps' nest in the potting shed? Someone should tell that lazy yard man that the cure for that is to tie a rag at the end of a long pole, set it afire and burn the devils out. Does that turtle still sun himself on the dead cypress knee by the pond? Is the old white swan still alive?

The trip here on that clattering old orbigator, *Noctule,* was more than unpleasant. In the stool sample line a man was brained as I stood by and watched. His crime? Slow bowels. They couldn't wait. Nothing but starch bars to eat and they crack open his skull with a billy club for slow bowels. It's an abomination.

As Ever,

Your Loving Grandmother

P.S. Don't be keeping company with either the butler or the yard man. Both of them are moral imbeciles. I intend to dismiss them as soon as I return.

A few weeks into Mildred's stay at Permanganate Island, she had visitors from the Administration. The pair arrived in a new Q-ped. Grasshoppers had burst green and yellow across the twin windshields. The belts and chains smoked as they cooled.

"Hello there," one of them called out. "May we come up?"

"What do you want? Who are you?"

"Administration. There could be a release in the works. We'd like to talk it over."

"By all means. Do come up. The steps are quite bad."

The pair were Raymo and Alana. "We're associate wardens," Raymo said.

"In charge of pardons," Alana added as they came breathless to the top of the stairs. Once inside, Raymo slid a document from his dusty briefcase. "Before we get started, Mrs. Balls, I want you to know that we know who you are."

Alana reached to shake Mildred's hand. "Your husband invented Jake powder. You're *that* Mildred Balls."

Raymo took her other hand. "Not to mention your own design for the Q-ped. Now I can say I've shaken the hand that held the hand of Jacob Balls and the pen that drew the first Q-ped."

Alana said, "What would the world be like if it weren't for those great ideas?"

Raymo began to pace, two or three steps in one direction, then two or three in the other. "Now, to get back to what I was saying. The Administration is willing to consider a fifty percent reduction in the normal time we keep infestation cases here, assuming we can get your parasites under control. And we think we just might be able to do that if we all pitch in and try hard. This would be in exchange for carrying out certain humanitarian tasks."

Alana and Raymo removed their duck cloth pedaling coats to reveal the typical uniforms of low-level Permanganate Administrators, their arm patches displaying the Permanganate Parasite Facility insignia—the letters PPF in black within a circle of stylized, red parasites.

Mildred hung their coats on a nail in the wall. "And what would be the nature of these duties?"

"You care for a group of stinkers, fourth-stage," Raymo said. "Retired donors, no longer useful in that way, but a lot of them are still surprisingly animated, so we want to build a pen out there where they'll be exposed to the elements night and day, year round. We'll want you to observe them and keep daily logs of their activities and behavior. You'll start with two or three of them."

"We'll replace any die-offs," Alana added. "They don't eat or drink much at this stage, so there's hardly any waste to dispose of. All you'll have to worry about is washing them once a week and rubbing them down with scented oil. Other than that they're pretty self sufficient."

Raymo continued, "The washing, as you also know, is mainly to keep the stink down. We'll leave you with ample supplies of soap, oil and sponges. Remember, their skin can parch and peel off if it gets too dry. That exposes muscle and bone to damaging sunlight, so be careful. And keeping detailed records is important." He produced a record book from his briefcase. "Everything goes right here."

"Don't laugh when you see what they're wearing," Alana chuckled. "It's mostly clinic-staff hand-me-downs. Stinkers have no sense of style whatsoever."

Mildred gave the offer some thought. Not only would it shorten her stay dramatically, she would have something to fill the hours. There would also be a limited degree of companionship, assuming she could communicate with stinkers at all. If frequent washing meant keeping the stink down, a year would pass quickly enough. Moreover, if her parasites proliferated beyond control, it was only a matter of time until she herself would need to be cared for. In that way helping out a few stinkers would be time well spent. "I'll sign on," she said. "It seems very fair."

Raymo gave the record book to her and she signed the agreement.

"One caution," Alana said. "Imps tend to gather when stinkers are in the area and they have been known to prey on them."

Raymo said, "They've given up grass and scum for a diet of stinker meat, what there is of it. No one knows why. A couple of them can chew up a downed stinker in a few minutes, head to toenails."

The Administrators put on their coats. "We'll be in touch at intervals to check on your stinkers," Alana said. "And, as a word of encouragement, we're on a fast track to finding a way to flush out those parasites. It's a matter of months. We've had several spontaneous cures lately. We're in the process of developing some theories about why as we speak."

"Be patient, Mrs. Balls," Raymo added. "Trustees will be here tomorrow to build the pens."

Alana had an afterthought. "One more thing. Is there a copy of the *Field Guide* here?"

"Yes, I found it in the closet."

"Have you been boning up on the Sayings?"

"I've memorized a few. 'Too much learning is a dangerous thing,' 'Travel is the serious part of frivolous lives,' 'The greatest affliction in life is never to be afflicted,' and, 'Excess of grief for a put-down stinker is an insult to the fully-alive.'"

"Only four?"

"I'm getting old. I don't have the memory I once had."

Alana said, "We'll try to be as patient as we can. You've got ninety-seven to go. Please, see that this gets done."

The next morning trustees arrived and went to work on the posts, wire and gate of the pen, finishing the job in a few hours. Meanwhile, Mildred sat near her window, keeping an eye on the trustees and writing another round of letters.

Dear Roe,

I hope to be back at the estate in less than a year. I've made an arrangement with the Administration. I'll be taking care of some donor stinkers in exchange for early release, depending on the level of my parasite load. I hope you and Ophelia are getting along. I've asked her not to lock you in the closet so much of the time. Make sure you take your medicine, practice your saw playing, and don't be putting any warm raisins in your sister's nose while she's asleep.

Your Grandmother

Dear Ophelia,

Make sure you have the butler give Roe his daily colonic. You know how he gets without it. And clean up after you shave him. Take him for walks. Above all, don't leave any fruit where he can get to it. I remember when you found him behind the stable forcing his little "worm" into a cored apple. That's a thing not to be repeated.

I'm praying that lazy yard man rakes the algae and duckweed from the pond. I don't want to come home to a stagnant little swamp. Tell Roe to go out to the potting shed in the afternoon and see if the lazy whelp is taking a nap on the peat bags. We catch him at that much too often.

I hope to be home sooner than expected. Until then, you are the "man" of the house in your grandmother's absence. Please fulfill your responsibilities to the estate and to Roe.

Finally, this is my message to you from captivity. Don't be such a shy, withering little flower. Advertise yourself. Dress prettily and have Roe take you to town. Dance with some of the fellows over at the Reverend's Templex. A few of them still have their heads screwed on and know not to kiss you. And you, of course, will not kiss anyone under any circumstances. To show affection, if you must, just touch the tips of your fingers to your tongue, then press them against the person's forehead.

I don't mean to be rushing you, but the sooner you mate, the sooner we'll have an offspring to nurse, play with and rear. I promise to be a full partner with you on the project. We'll build you and the child a nice little cozy cottage on the estate grounds.

All of this begs the question, though, which is, will the parasites die before I do? I hope the answer is yes. I hope there's a way to expel them, every last one and all their eggs.

Remember me in your nightly meditations.

With all my affection,
Grandmother

Sealing the letters and stamping them, she called down to the trustees. "Please, can you take these letters back to Administration for posting?"

One of them said, "We build pens for stinks. That's all we know about."

Mildred waved the letter in the air. "Isn't there a letter-post there, at Administration?"

"Yeah, there's one."

"And you're going back there, aren't you?"

"Yeah."

"And you won't just drop these off at the post?"

"Nope. Can't do that. All we do is build pens for stinks. If we did anything else, they'd spank us till our rumps were purple."

"I'd pay you, but they took every buck I had."

A third trustee said, "Don't you boys know who that is? That's Mildred Balls. She's rich as God. Her old man owned the recipe for making Jake, and she invented the Q-ped."

"Please, will you take these letters to Administration?"

"Shit on you, you rich old cow. Look where your money got you."

The day following completion of the pen, a pedal truck appeared with three stinkers asleep in the bed under a blanket of leaves and straw. Mildred threw on her house robe and stood in the doorway. Two trustees got out of the truck in the midst of an argument.

"You lazy clump of shit! Who did all the pedaling? My legs are killing me."

"Who got out and oiled them chains every couple miles? It was me, slopehead!"

"Stop that fighting!" Mildred shouted.

One of the trustees shook his fist at her. "Stay out of other people's business!" He poked the stinkers with sharp sticks to wake them. "Here you go, lady, three old stinks in sore need of a good washing."

The weary stinkers, all males, climbed out of the truck's bed and were prodded into the pen. All wore soiled, wrinkled business suits, outlandish ties and mis-matched footwear. Once locked into the pen, they lay beside one another in the dirt and began to snore.

The two trustees got back in the truck and resumed their bickering.

"This time, I oil and you pedal, you rotten son of a bitch."

"Kiss my ass till your nose breaks off, you god-damned moron."

Mildred went inside and got the letters to her grandchil-dren. "Can you take these with you and post them? I don't want to wait a month."

The driver's head angled out of the window. "We haul stinkers, lady. We don't carry no mail."

"Please, can you make an exception?"

"A what?"

"Just this once. Take my letters to Administration. My grandchildren. They worry about me."

"Okay, one time. Next time, wait for the mail pickup."

"I will."

"You swear?"

"I do."

The other trustee trudged halfway up the stairs. "My legs hurt. Throw 'em down. I'll catch 'em."

Mildred tied the letters with an imp-hair strand from her sweater in hopes they would stay together, then tossed them to the trustee with a flick of her wrist. The catch was success-ful and the trustee backed down. "Okay, that's it. No more schleppin' mail, lady. You know what I'm sayin'?"

"Oh, yes."

The truck moved slowly down the narrow road that led west, and the quiet returned. Mildred stood by the window as the sun set and kept an eye on the stinkers until it was too dark to see them. The door had no lock and she went to bed fretful. Why, she wondered, would the Administration send her three males?

It seemed thoughtless. Surely females would have been a better choice for an old woman to handle. She had read many times in the papers of criminality among late-stage stinkers. It was not unheard of for them to commit assault, rape, even murder.

But the night passed without incident. Though Mildred could hear imps shrieking in the distance, they hadn't yet picked up the scent of her stinkers, who slept peacefuly together on the ground. Their snoring was something of a comfort, like far away thunder, and Mildred awoke with the first sunlight that reached her face. When she opened the window, a small cloud of urpflanz pollen blew in. "Autumn's on the way," she said to herself.

The stinkers were walking around the perimeter of their pen, hands in pockets, searching the ground, as if something of value, or importance, had been lost. They looked up in her direction for a moment.

Mildred cupped her small mouth with arthritic hands and shouted, "Yoo-hooo, fellows? I'll be down there after break-fast and give you baths."

First, she would have to collect her stool sample. After working the noisy pump handle until the tank of the commode was full, she sat down with a fresh tongue depressor, emptied her bowels, and lifted out the required amount.

The odor of the stinkers seeped under the tower's loose siding and through the window, curbing Mildred's appetite. She was able to get down only a small plug of imp meat and a few bites of starch bar before putting on her rags, tying her long white hair into a bun atop her head and slipping on a pair of leaky rubber boots she found in the closet.

As she walked toward the door with an armload of washing supplies, scented oil and a pan of water, she felt a sting on the bottom of her foot. It was not particularly painful, less so than a bee sting, so she stepped down hard, crushed whatever had bitten her, and carried on with her obligations. She recognized the possibility that it might have been a fiddle-back, but chose to file the thought away.

When she got to the pen, the stinkers were continuing to walk in circles, policing the perimeter of the pen. "You stinkers," she called, stepping into the pen. "Do you have names?"

All three stopped walking at once, but continued looking downward. One of them said, "Spanish Johnny." Another mumbled, "Percy Chips." The third, whose shoes were on the wrong feet, grumbled, "They call me Side Porch."

"'Cause they found him under somebody's side porch half-buried under trash and dirt," Spanish Johnny offered.

Percy Chips said, "Me, I started getting stiff when I was playing a lot of poker in a Pisstown slum. Got stiffer and stiffer and deader and deader. Now look at me."

Spanish Johnny told of coming north to pick persimmons, then being shifted to a donor farm, where he succumbed in a desperate state of mind. "They found me in an old wooden water tower. Stunk up the whole town's water most of a year. People went around in clothes that smelled like they'd been washed in a sewer ditch."

"Well, then," she told them, "My name is Mildred Balls. Let's get you washed, one at a time. Take off your clothes, please."

In unison, all three kicked off their shoes, peeled off socks, loosened belts and lowered trousers. Spanish Johnny gasped, but did not cry out in pain when a strip of hide that was stuck to his underpants came off, exposing a swath of moist, red muscle tissue. Another accident occurred when Side Porch removed the snap-brim cap he was wearing and took a divot of scalp with it. And when Percy Chips's trousers fell, it was apparent that his entire sexual apparatus had been excised and the incision left to heal without benefit of stitching. It was an ugly, suppurating wound.

"Yeah, go ahead and gawk," he said.

The others pointed to similar evidence of excisions on themselves. "They took our manhood away is what they did," Side Porch said. "Worse, we're not dead enough to burn yet."

"I got maybe a pound of liver left," Chips said. "I lost my stomach, thyroid, one eye, all my toenails and half my brain."

Side Porch and Spanish Johnny had donated kidneys, spleens, lungs and teeth, they said.

"I'm sorry about all that, fellows, but my job is to wash you on a regular basis. Now, all of you kneel down on all fours and let me get you wet." When the stinkers complied, without objection or hesitation, Mildred sloshed water over their frail, withered backs and began soaping them up, being very careful not to puncture or tear their paper-thin skin. When the washing was done, the stinkers stood in a close circle and let her rub them with scented oil.

Side Porch said, "You got the parasite, Mildred? Is that why they put you way out here?"

"Yes."

"That's bad," Chips said. "By the time they're through, you'll be a bag of bones."

"Hell, I had them bad when I was third-stage," Side Porch said. "Got to where they were coming out in my hanky when I blew my nose. I could feel them moving around in my head. I'd shit a bucket full every morning. Then they went away when I got to be fourth-stage."

Spanish Johnny admitted to becoming infested when he was in the Reverend's Guard during the occupation of Pisstown. "When the Chaos ended, a first-stage female came up and gave me a kiss. That's how I got the parasite. I tried every remedy that rumor delivered to me, including moxibustion and urpmilk enemas, but it just got worse."

Mildred told them she had high hopes of finding a way to cure herself.

When the stinkers put their clothes back on and returned to walking in circles and searching the ground, Mildred could no longer keep her curiosity at bay. "Are you fellows looking for something?"

"No, Miss," Spanish Johnny said, "We like to get dizzy and faint. It's the way we have fun."

"Good day, then."

"There's a full moon coming tonight," Percy Chips said. "We go crazy sometimes when that happens."

"But don't you worry, Miss," Spanish Johnny said. "There's no way any of us could get up those stairs. We're way too stiff in the joints."

Side Porch took a few rigid, awkward steps. "See, most of mine are fused. It's a damn good thing I don't feel much pain, or this would be pure agony."

"I won't worry, then," Mildred said, closing the gate.

"This day'll never dawn again," Chips said.

Side Porch spun around like a top, but slowly. "We'll see what tomorrow brings." He fell to the ground then. Chips and Johnny picked him up.

"He's all right," Johnny said.

"Be very careful when you fall," Mildred warned as she closed the gate. "There are hungry imps in the area. This fence won't keep them out."

When the moon was up and the haze had lifted, Mildred watched the stinkers from her window. They circled the pen dozens of times before Percy Chips crumbled in a dead faint. Moments later, she heard the squealing of wild imps and watched in disgust as two of them burrowed under the fence wire and tore away most of one buttock and part of Chips's face before Side Porch was able to chase them off. "I'm okay," Chips said. "I don't feel anything. I don't see any blood."

Mildred's attention was suddenly drawn to a feeling of pressure, an itch, and a subtle throbbing in her heel. When she sat on the side of her cot and removed the boot, a flattened brown spider tumbled out. When her knee sock came off, she saw a foot that was puffy and enflamed. A conspicuous target-like bite mark lay on that part just beneath her long second toe, and rings of disturbed flesh

35

spread outward from the site. The dead spider was a dark, long-legged one, and there was the unmistakable marking of a fiddle on its back.

Dear Roe and Ophelia,

I am in quite a fix. A poisonous spider has bitten me and my foot is swollen all the way to the ankle. Walking on it is too painful to bear and I don't have anything to make into a suitable crutch. Where am I going to find a physician to cut out all the necrotic flesh that comes with these bites? Here I am, three stinkers to take care of, and I can't walk. Another day or two and their odor will begin to sicken me further. I don't think I've ever been in such a pickle before. This will have to be cut short as I'm growing weak and my fingers are too numb to write. How I long to be home again.

Your Ailing Grandmother

Three.

Nowadays, you aren't necessarily sent to Permanganate Island Prison because you've violated any law. Anyone could be ordered there as a side effect of the shifting process. Because of the complex stochastic methods used in calculating the shifts, some unfortunates have to be "side-shifted," most often to an out-of-the-way or isolated place like a prison island or watch tower. In urban areas it could be a warehouse, a derelict theater, or an abandoned building.

In a show of sympathy, the Reverend spent an hour with a sick stinker yesterday. She had vomited everything for a month except piquant foods. She told him her physician had prescribed aqua chloroformant, spirits of menthol, willywhack and urpmeal. Yet she had not gotten better. For eight years before this, she had suffered with arthritis deformans. Her hands were nothing but clubs. "I was once very pretty," she said. "I was admired by the whole bailiwick for my beautiful hair."

When the meeting was over, the Reverend said that her complaints had led him to reconsider drugless healing. "Since the beginning of homeopathy, followed by chiropody, osteopathy and chiropractic, drugless healing has taken tremendous steps forward," he said to reporters. "When one realizes there are other ways of healing, they will not be slow in forsaking the nauseating draughts medicine offers."

A fondness for pickled lips has led to the arrest of a Kootie Fiyo, a stinker known to be a trader in tooth gold and a vicious biter. Fiyo was just leaving the impeteria in South Pisstown when two Guards entered. The proprietor said, "That stink can eat more imp lips than I can heap in front of him."

The Guards remembered receiving a report from Bum Bay that a stinker of Fiyo's description was wanted there on an infectious biting charge, and that the suspect's most conspicuous affection was for pickled lips.

Fiyo was arrested after a scuffle, during which one of the Guards was bitten on his face, neck and hand and is now under observation at Pisstown's Pasteur Clinic. The other Guard escaped with minor bruises and abrasions. Fiyo was rushed through the judication process at the Templex and just as quickly sent to a dentist to have all his teeth extracted. Should the bitten Guard die, Fiyo will probably hang.

Lovesick stinkers have set up a spooning area in the alleyway between the Radiola and the Gons Hotel. Flocks of them are a nightly disturbance to the hotel's guests. There are always two or three couples under every window, spooning away, and their shrieks awaken the guests.

The Reverend told the City Moon, *"I can't say that I am opposed to stinkers coupling publicly, if they so desire, but they have no right doing it in the proximity of a hotel," and promised to use his influence to keep the unwanted lovemakers at bay.*

Reverend Hooker tells of the time his body became the dwelling place of an outsize parasite. Physicians were consulted and by various methods they tried without success to kill the large parasite. It was hoped the monster would come out of its own accord, via some natural passage such as the mouth or anus. Once when Hooker ate urpflanz honey, it crawled into his mouth and parted his lips with its head. It was without eyes and its color was green.

One of the Reverend's assistants grasped the head and part of the body and attempted to pull it out altogether, but the slimy thing slipped through her hands and down the Reverend's throat as though it had been greased. Often thereafter, Hooker ate honey in hopes of the parasite again making its appearance, but it never came up farther than his gullet.

A year ago, while in bed, he was awakened in his sleep by something crawling across his chest. He screamed and the parasite quickly drew itself back down his throat. Late Saturday he was seized with a choke, which continued periodically during the night, and early Sunday morning the parasite slithered out of his mouth several inches. With great presence of mind, he closed his teeth on the repulsive creature and ran to his assistant, who succeeded in entirely relieving him of the unwelcome tenant, which was fifteen inches long, and died a few minutes after being in the air. The Reverend's stomach has refused to hold food except in liquid form since the parasite came out. For months he grew weaker and weaker, until physicians thought he would die as a result of getting rid of the parasite, which had made his internal anatomy its home for so many years.

It has been revealed in the Reverend's newsletter that he would like to speak to the ones who hid a large syringe filled with what he believes to have been imp-liver extract, pointed upward in his Q-ped seat. He sat on the needle and the pressure of his body operated the plunger. He did not get the full injection, but did become ill.

A.J. Beals, Pisstown mortician, will take likenesses of the sick or deceased. He employs beeswax and plaster techniques similar to those used by the Macedonians. He asks that patrons contact him immediately upon the death of their loved ones, before rigor sets in. In the case of illness, he will take action when all hope is lost.

I went down to Camp Legion today, to the stinker fish pavilion on the banks of the National Canal. The place was swarming with blackflies of every size. Just above one of the metal tubs where Canal fish were being boiled, hung a sign emblazoned with the Hookerite credo, "We Die That We May Die No More."

Mose Howard, chief of the crew, pulled a small section from the stomach of each fish as it went by him on a hand-cranked conveyor belt. He whiffed it and passed judgment. If the odor was strong enough, the fish continued to the cooking room. If the fish was too fresh, it was yanked from the belt and thrown back into the Canal. Mose complained that he was plagued with aching neck muscles because of the constant intake of putrid air, averaging one smell every two and a half seconds. Mose says he smells thirty to thirty-five tons of fish every shift, working from fourteen to sixteen hours a day. He can sniff more than twelve thousand tons of fish every year without once inhaling a fly.

As a boy, Mildred's grandson, Roe, was housed in a rickety wooden structure on the grounds of the Balls estate, well away from the main compound and hidden by brambles and brush. The hastily built structure was an oven in summer and an icebox in winter. The yard man advised him to dig a small trench around the building and fill it with tooth powder to keep out rodents, adders and most walking insects. This he did, and nothing walking or slithering entered, but flying things had free access through a number of broken windows and things that hopped could occasionally take advantage of a door left open.

The National Canal ran cold and babbling through the property and Roe liked to fish it. One afternoon, in an effort to throw the line far into the stream, where the grandest fish lay, he slung it high into the air, with the result that the hook, sinkers and line lodged in a tree thirty-five feet tall. He climbed the tree to release the tackle. When he reached the limb on which the line had become entangled, a whippoorwill was fast to the hook, the barb having penetrated the eye socket. The bird had gone for his grub in error and had suffered the consequences.

When Roe brought the whippoorwill home in his creel and showed it to his grandfather, explaining how it happened that he'd caught a bird while fishing, Jacob's reply was, as it often was, off subject. "Too bad it wasn't an oyster," he said. "I did love the oysters I once harvested from that Canal. Even the famed oysters of Britain, devoured by the Romans, cannot be compared to the once-great oyster of the National Canal, which weighed two pounds and always contained a good pearl."

"The pearls're all gone now," Mildred said. "But I have a trunk full of chokers as mementos."

"Should I tell him now?" Jacob asked.

Mildred lowered her eyes. "Yes, this is the right time. We don't want to keep it secret."

"All right, young man, I'm in the middle of a scandal. It happened during a quarrel in the saloon of Bartholomew Donohue, at No. 9 Varick Street. I slapped a female stinker across the face. In falling, her head struck an iron radiator, and she was completely dead in a few minutes. By the time an officer arrived, Donohue had washed the woman's face and brushed her ragged clothing clean."

"The other patrons and your grandfather," Mildred said,

"discussed things and agreed that what had happened was merely an accident. The woman slipped on a spot of spilled Jake and fell, they agreed to say. But the officer would have none of that and charges were brought."

"Fleecing the rich is what they're all about, this Administration. Just because I own a brewery or two, they'll be trying to send me to Permanganate Island or Indian Apple, or some other smelly hole on the slightest excuse."

"What will Grandfather do, Grandmother?"

"The charges won't be proven. But for the meantime, we'll be traveling."

Jacob sat in a soft chair and lit an urpflanz cigar. "You don't know much about your grandfather's past, do you, Roe?"

"Very little, to tell you the truth."

Jacob dusted ash from his lapels with a starched hand-kerchief. "There will be revelations about that and more at another time."

"We'll be back when this all blows over," Mildred said.

Jacob crossed his legs, his patent pump glinting for a moment in the candlelight. "As a matter of fact we'll sail tomorrow aboard the *Titanic*, past the Cape and around the Horn, as far from the warring factions as we can get. A nasty Chaos has broken out in Pisstown and it could spread here to the exurbs any day. I hope you'll devote more energy to maturation from now on. Your grandmother and I will not be holding your hand forever."

"What about me, Grandmother? What happens to me?"

"I've asked your sister to take care of you."

"Seems like joining the Reverend's Guard would be the decent thing for a lazy lad like you to do," Jacob said.

"I'll enlist tomorrow," Roe sighed.

"Toodle-oo," Mildred said. "We promise to send you cards with regularity."

The next day, Roe enlisted. The day after that he was biv-
ouacked somewhere in the Fertile Crescent, where he nearly
met disaster when a railcar, heavily laden and running on the
downgrade at top speed, approached a spot where he and
other soldiers sat resting. Behind the railcar came a rolling
platform carrying a load of porous clay zeer jars. The conveyance was built this way so that the heavy jars might catch the
rush of air and thus cool the contents to drinking temperature. As the car rounded a curve, one of the zeers toppled
and struck the soldier sitting next to Roe with full force,
crushing his skull. The worst Roe suffered was a drenching.

Other than the time he volunteered for a risky mission,
the remainder of his military service was unexceptional and
dull. Reverend Hooker had come to the bivouac to deliver
a message to the newly enlisted troops, who assembled in
a large tent. "Listen, men," he said, "striped adders are so
thick in a pasture on one of my farms that they have taken
to milking my imps. And when they are active at this, there
is a distinctly pungent odor. Last evening I found that every
imp in a herd of nine hundred had been milked. I camou-
flaged myself and watched the pasture. Every minute or two,
I saw an adder crawl up an imp's leg and begin to milk the
animal. And men, let me add that those same imps rarely
grin when I palm their teats. Now, the point of the tale is
this—I need volunteers to hunt down the adders and kill
them. It's dangerous work as these slithery things will strike
with deadly effect. Let's have a show of hands, then. Who'll
volunteer to save the milk supply?"

Roe volunteered. It promised to be more engaging than
sitting in a tent all day and night with the steamy rain pelt-
ing down. Taking the next available wagon, he reported for
duty at the Reverend's imp farm. The operation proceeded
in a straightforward way, beginning with a few remarks from
Hooker. "Listen up, men. This is the way this will be done.
You'll line up side by side in the nude and you'll cross the

entire pasture. Every other man will carry one of these rubber udders filled with imp's milk, letting it hang by his side." He took a full udder from an assistant and demonstrated the best way to dangle it. "When the adders begin to climb the man's leg, I want the soldier next to him to snatch up that serpent with one of these gloves." He held up a pair of elbow-length gauntlets. "And put it in a sack like this." He held up a burlap bag with a drawstring. "Now, no matter what safety precautions we take, some of you will be bitten, some of you will die, a few will suffer lifelong from the effects of the bite. To date no antivenin has been made available. So, in closing, let me wish you the best of luck. I've never seen such a lineup of finely made men."

By random selection, Roe ended up one of the udder carriers. To the soldier next to him, he said, "Please, act quickly, don't let one bite me." As soon as the line moved into the high grass, adders began winding up leg after leg, including Roe's. "Get it! Get it!" he screeched.

The soldier reached for the adder as quickly as humanly possible, yet it was too late. Roe was bitten on one of his testicles. Though the bite caused swelling to the point that he was anchored to his cot for five days, feet propped up, applying cold packs, very little venom had been injected and physicians said he would recover without permanent damage.

Four.

An imp herder working one of the Reverend's meadows is fit to be tied. He found his most productive female dead in her pen yesterday. The belly was scissored open, the teats cut, the heart carried off. The herder wants to blame stinkers for this latest raid on his stock. The incident is doubly sorrowful, coming so soon after the same herder discovered the wings of his favorite banty imp nailed to the stump of an oak. Neighbors testify that he now spends his time stalking the reaches of the Reverend's property, pistol drawn, so anxious to shoot a stinker that he has accidentally killed three of his best stud imps.

A stinker using a bow and arrow bagged a wild imp today in front of the Radiola Theater in full view of horrified patrons, who watched him dress it with surgical precision, cube and salt the meat, wrap it in burlap, and run north, leaving behind a mound of gristle and bone.

Because the Reverend believes that music is the fourth material want of the stinker, he has put in effect ordinances requiring them to whistle while they work and to toot kazoos during breaks. Knee-slapping, spoon-rattling, drumming, trumpeting and blowing the short horn are also mandated. As a result, Bum Bay has become a noisy circus of tone-deaf stinkers trying to comply with the ordinance.

A metal pontoon of some kind was being drawn by pedal cart down the main streets of Pisstown. It measured six foot by six. A hole in its outer plating admitted a tangle of colored wires and leaked a pine-scented, pleasant smelling gas, one which, if inhaled even at a distance of a city block, brought on a lingering giddiness, a stagger, and a closure of the throat. The cylinder had apparently been at the bottom of the National Canal for some time, judging by the crust of slime and barnacles.

Out of the crowd that formed to watch the strange looking object pass, one valorous soul went up and stroked it kindly, as though it were a living thing. He did this despite warnings from the Home Guards escorting the cylinder at a safe distance and lived only a few moments after the thoughtless act. In autopsy it was discovered that his lungs and trachea were coated with a thick layer of parasites, presumably carried in with the leaking gas, which thusfar has defied chemical analysis.

One of the Reverend's closest held secrets was revealed today by the City Moon *after an American business-woman said she saw a bright globe rise aloft and traverse portions of the sky above a factory which produces chloride of lime, and continue until it paused high above the Bum Bay Straits. She offered to swear an affidavit in substantiation of what she saw. It hovered blue and bulbous, she said, and a sterilizing light seemed to be cast from its underparts.*

"I guess the word is out," the Reverend told the paper. "The woman saw a prototype of a small moon that heals, a medicinal moon. My scientists and I have been hard at work on this project for many years. The moon is intended to cleanse the atmosphere of parasite spores. I see these globes someday stationed over every city, town and waiting camp in the land."

Stinkers are said to dote on a mixture of urpflanz pulp and sweetened urpmilk. To that end they have learned to connect a crank with a dasher in a churn and set the container in a pan of Canal ice and salt, to produce a delicious concoction they call ice butter, which they vend from three-wheeled carts at a half-buck a cup, under gaily colored umbrellas.

These peddlers, citizens have been cautioned, are rich sources of parasite infestation, dysentery, diphtheria and sundry bacterial infections, as most of the ice butter is manufactured in unsanitary homes, with unclean hands.

While most of the household workers had departed when Mildred Balls left for Permanganate Island, two remained: Red Cane, an unreliable and moody man who performed the services of both a butler and a cook, and Reuben Peters, the yard man.

One morning Red prepared lunch in the kitchen downstairs, then brought it up to Ophelia. "I've stuffed a few pastry shells with mushrooms and urpmilk and baked them for you, an old recipe of your grandmother's I found under the cooking stove."

"Thank you so much," Ophelia said, dragging her chair to a window to take advantage of the warm sunlight as she ate. "Look at that. The postman is emptying his bowels again. There's his Q-ped in the driveway. I see him by the pond."

David Ohle

The postman squatted in a thicket of wild urpflanz, whistling as he wiped himself with pages torn from the *City Moon.*

"Hey, you!" Ophelia barked. "This place may look a shambles, but it's not abandoned. I could go out for a walk and step in that."

The postman hiked up his pants. "There's a letter from your grandmother." He waved it in the air. "You're lucky I didn't wipe with it."

"Give it to Red. And if you do that again, I'll take it up with one of Hooker's legal wigs. I'll file a peace bond. This is just too much."

"It's from Permanganate Island. She infested?"

"That's none of your business!" Ophelia shouted.

"And if I catch you leaving those smelly brown parcels on this property again," Red warned from the servant's entrance, "I'll strangle you. The smell catches the night breeze and blows in the windows. It brings flies. You've probably contaminated the pond, too, you lout!"

The postman climbed into the Q-ped and strapped himself in. "Here's what I think of you kind of people." He poked a finger into his mouth and pretended to vomit as he pedaled down the lane.

Red brought Ophelia the letter from Mildred. "There's your mail. Now it's time for my nap in the sunroom. Please don't disturb me until supper time." He closed the door softly and tiptoed down the creaky stairs.

Ophelia read the letter, then responded:

Dear Grandmother,

I am in receipt of your letter to Roe and me, though I have to tell you, Roe got his shifting orders. I came to tears when I watched from an upper window

48

as he left home. He carried his saw and bow in a canvas bag over one shoulder, a duffel bag that I had packed for him over the other, and a little impskin satchel for medicine and personal items, including a bottle of homemade cough syrup. Don't worry, I followed your recipe exactly: one measure of honey, one ounce hydrate of turpentine, persimmon juice and a generous spoon of Jake powder.

So sorry to hear they've confined you that way without your creature comforts. Even though it is springtime here, I haven't been singing much. The hydrangea did bloom, but sparingly. The soil, I think, has been tainted by seepage from Peters's latrine. Incidentally, you'll want to know, he burned himself when he tried your method of getting rid of the wasps in the potting shed. The flaming rag fell right in his face and set his hair on fire, then the wool of his sweater. He was flaming head to shoulders when he plunged into the pond. Other than burned-off eyebrows and hair, he isn't terribly disfigured. In fact, Red thinks he looks better. Yes, the swan is still alive, barely. The neck droops, it falls often. It doesn't have long.

As to me, I just pass the time waiting for my shifting orders. When I'm gone, we'll have only Red and the yard man to care for the place. Of course, they could be shifted, too, then what?

Love,
Ophelia

Red rushed upstairs one morning just after dawn and bit Ophelia on the wrists and face, vicious bites that left welts and little scabbings for weeks. "Next time," he said, "I'll cut your head half-off with a bread knife."

Sitting up in bed, Ophelia asked, "What have I done? I've done nothing."

49

"There was a muddy print on the Oriental carpet in the foyer. It was yours. That rug was your grandmother's favorite. I spent half the night cleaning it."

"If Peters would fix the walkway it wouldn't be such a bog."

Red's body sagged as if a current had been suddenly cut off. "It was an impulse. An urge I could not rein in. I'm so, so sorry. I can be as unpredictable as the weather, a sudden storm on a sunny day. The fury often comes after a period of serene, languid calm. Whatever the mood, it typically lasts from one sunrise to another."

"Is that a reason to bite me? What if I'm infested now?"

"I'm parasite-free. Don't be alarmed."

Red dressed Ophelia's wounds, first applying tincture of Mercurochrome, then a layer of French clay. "These things are beyond understanding or explanation. You won't tell your grandmother, will you?"

"Do anything like that again and I will."

Backing from the room, Red said, "I'll get your breakfast now."

That night Ophelia sat upright in bed, nursing her wounds, chewing on a plug of imp meat and drinking a bottle of Jake. A half-moon, prominent in a close corner of the sky, looked low enough to bounce off hilltops and threw a milky light into the room. It was as perfect as nights ever got for thinking things over.

What would happen to the estate if her shifting orders came? It would be left in the care of the butler and the yard man and that would be the death-knell. It would be overtaken by roving stinkers and displaced shiftees before the persimmon trees turned brown. When the thought of persimmons crossed her mind, she made a mental note to write a real note to the yard man, asking him to pick a bucket of them and bring it to Red, who would bake some of them in a pie and make jam of the rest.

She then gave thought to avoiding the shift by going to the Balls summer home on Square Island. She could lay low there awhile. She could claim, truthfully, that she was away when her papers came and never saw them.

Red burst in suddenly, without knocking, unlinking Ophelia's chain of thought, and sat cross-legged on the floor. "I haven't been well," he said.

"Neither have I." Ophelia displayed her now-inflamed bites. "Look what you did to me."

"I've already extended apologies. What more do you expect?"

"What did you come in here for? I'm busy thinking things over."

"I have a case of the heebie-jeebies." He went to the window. "Look, there's the all-night pedal tram to Bum Bay. If they shift me somewhere, I guess I'll be on it one of these days."

"I hope you aren't shifted any time soon, Red, because I'm thinking of going to the Island for a few weeks and you'll be left in charge, you and Peters. If my shifting papers come, which I expect they will very soon, leave them in the box."

"Yes, Miss. We'll keep the stinks away, too."

"Good. If you let the first one get a foothold here, it's ants on a sticky bun."

"That's right, Miss."

"You can go now. I'm getting sleepy. And tell Peters to pick a bucket of persimmons tomorrow."

"G'night, Miss. I'll go out and tell him right now. He and I are developing a close friendship."

When the sun reached mid-heaven the next morning, Red brought Ophelia her breakfast. "Here's your starch bar and urpflanz tea. Anything else? I'm off to the potting shed again. Last night I saw some tasty-looking mushrooms sprouting from the peat. I'll be back with some to cook for dinner."

"Yes, fine."

In an hour, after Ophelia had napped and gone downstairs for a little sit in the sunroom, Red returned with a sack of mushrooms, knocking the mud from his boots with a dandelion fork. "Look what I've got for dinner." White and puffy, they smelled like starch, and fat little beetles were feeding on them.

"Yes, that's nice. Now, Red, for your information, I'll be leaving for Square Island in a few days. Please oil the pedal chains and grease the bearings in my Q-ped. It's been put up so long it must be rusting by now."

"Very well, Miss. Count on me to keep an eye on things while you're gone. Supper at seven. We're having eel stew tonight just the way your grandmother cooks it. Peters caught them this morning in the Canal. They're very fresh."

"Mmmmmm."

Carrying the thought of a nice eel stew upstairs with her, Ophelia lay down in her tub to bathe. When she turned on the spigot, little green clumps of duckweed and a few minnows came out with the water. When the tub was full, she felt like she was sitting in an aquarium. She added scented oil to the water to mask its earthy scent. She tried to shave her legs, but what was left of the bar of soap wouldn't make decent suds. With the first stroke of the razor, one that once belonged to her grandfather, she cut her ankle and bled.

When the bath was over and she had dried off with a freshly laundered towel, a rusty film covered her body. Her face and hands appeared gray. When she went down for dinner, feeling poorly, she found the dining room lit by candles and the table set with her grandmother's china and silverware. A pitcher of Jake and a mushroom pie had been carefully positioned between two crystal vases that sprouted fresh geraniums. All the chairs but two, placed side by side, had been taken away.

In the kitchen, Red stood hunched at the sink, scrubbing pots and pans. His cheeks were either rosier than usual or the rest of his face more pale. "I'll be there in a moment. I have to get this pan scrubbed. The whole process is making me very anxious."

"Stay calm, Red." Ophelia drank a glass of Jake, hoping it would settle her stomach. "I do appreciate all you've done towards this meal, all the trouble you've gone to, but I'm out of sorts tonight. The bathwater was awful. It made me sick."

"Miss, if I've told Peters once, I've told him a thousand times, to clean out that standpipe by the pond. That's what's getting into the plumbing, it's that pond water. I've told him, I've said, 'There's snakes in that pond. How would you like one in your bathtub with you?' That's what I told him."

"All right. I'll see if I can keep some stew down, but not the pie, thank you."

"Oh, no. You must have some pie. I demand it." Red waltzed in with a steaming bowl and ladle and sat shoulder to shoulder with Ophelia, then sliced the pie. A creamy sauce poured out while the mushroom chunks remained beneath the burned crust. Little or no attempt had been made to cull for beetles. Their parts floated freely in the sauce along with flecks and strands of peat.

"I don't mean to be suspicious, Red, but what sort of mushrooms are those? Are they safe to eat?"

"Oh, yes. Peters cultivates them. In a week, here we are, a whole pie full. Eat the bugs, too. They feed on the mushrooms. That's where the flavor is."

"Just a small piece, please."

Red served Ophelia a much larger piece than she wanted. "Eat all of it, and fast. That's the best way. Really, the only way. You might as well throw it out to the imps as eat just a little, or too slowly."

Rather than risk an outburst of anger on Red's part, Ophelia ate a forkful of the pie, which was refreshingly flavorless, except for the beetles, which crunched with a tiny release of peppery fluid. She ate another, larger forkful, and then was able to finish the slice as Red stood behind her saying, again and again, "Hurry now. Hurry up and get it down. Hurry up and get it down. Hurry now."

"It wasn't as bad as I thought," Ophelia said, wiping a beetle from the corner of her lip.

Red asked, "Mind if I make a confession to you before you leave?"

"Of course not, Red."

"Did you notice the smear of rouge on my sunken cheeks?"

"No, I hadn't."

"I'm wearing some of your grandmother's underthings, too."

"Just don't soil them, that's all."

"I'll be so-so careful not to. That's a promise." He ladled a bowl of the eel stew. "Is that enough, Miss?"

"Plenty."

"When you leave I'll pack the rest in jars. You can take them along in a basket."

"That would be ducky."

By morning, after a long, deep sleep, Ophelia felt fit, light and energetic. She went to the window after hearing nervous laughter from below and looked down toward the potting shed. Peters knelt at a stump, stretching the swan's neck over it, and Red raised an axe and lopped off its head. Peters then nailed its feet to the side of the potting shed to let it bleed.

Red looked toward the house. "Good morning, Miss! I'm going to bake this old bird for your going-away supper."

"That was Grandmother's pet."

"I know, Miss, but you can see it's on its last legs. Isn't it best to make some use of it, before it goes off somewhere to die?" Peters said.

"Grandmother won't agree, but I don't have time to worry about this. I need my colonic. Will you give it to me, Red?"

"I'd be honored. Let me do this plucking and we'll get right to it."

Ophelia searched through her grandmother's toiletries for an enema bag and a bar of floating soap, which she had little trouble locating. She took them into the bathroom, placed them in the sink, sat on the stool and read an insert in a copy of the *City Moon*. The piece was written by Hooker himself, using the nom de plume Dr. Christopher Nyrop, on the subject of kissing: "It is well-known that kissing is the main culprit when it comes to spreading parasites. Therefore I feel it appropriate to explore the subject more closely. The first requisite of a kiss is a mouth. A sucking movement of the lip muscles, accompanied by an audible sound that varies in length and intensity. But, this alone does not constitute a kiss. You may also hear the same sound when an imp driver calls his imps. No, it is a kiss only when it is used to convey a feeling of affection and when the lips come in brief or sustained contact with a living creature or object."

When Red came in, he was wearing rubber boots and an apron from the potting shed, and was holding a shower cap in his hand. Though his mood had become sour, the swan feather clinging to his nose gave him a clownish look. "I'm not in the mood for this," he said.

"You certainly look dressed for it."

"When I said I would do it, I was in another mood. I'm like a werewolf. Have you noticed? I think it was last night's moon. Some magnetic effect beyond my control."

"I'll do it myself, then. It wouldn't be the first time. You just calm down."

"No, I insist. Let's get started."

Red filled the bag with warm, soapy water, and oiled the nozzle. He flexed his fingers and slid on a pair of dirty work-gloves. "All right, Miss, climb into the tub and bend over."

Ophelia stepped high and into the cold porcelain tub and braced herself against slippage. Red inserted the nozzle without looking directly at her anus. He merely pushed on it until it found home. Ophelia stifled an outcry by biting her lip.

"Sorry again, Miss. I've always been something of a klutz. My past is full of holes. I may have been born in Lund, near the Alps. But what did I do when I wandered away from the Q-ped factory one day? I've always wondered that."

Ophelia's impactment broke loose and a few dark, granular turds dropped into the tub. "Thank you, Red. That's a relief."

"Let me clean up now. Go wipe yourself."

Ophelia stepped out of the tub, planting her toes first on the mat, then the rest of her foot. She sat on the commode to wipe, using a little unguent afterward to soothe her bottom.

"Will you help me douche, now?"

"Oh, yes, Miss, I'd be glad to. As soon as I'm finished cleaning up."

When the bathroom sparkled again, and the douching was done, Red said he was going downstairs to begin browning the swan in fat.

"Thank you for helping me."

"It's a pleasure, Miss."

"You were gentle but patient and thorough."

"For the douche, I diluted the vinegar with rosewater. Wasn't that a nice touch?"

"It was. Thank you again."

Ophelia lay in her bed for an hour or two, reading the *City Moon*, until the rich cooking fumes that drifted up the stairwell, along with the sizzle and pop of hot fat, lulled her to sleep. During the nap she dreamed she was in a pedal tram station dressed in a gray and blue military uniform and lugging a fully packed duffel bag. Another soldier stopped her and asked, "Which train to the Chaos?" For a moment, in the dream, Ophelia was perplexed. She thought all trains went there.

She awoke famished. With cleaned-out bowels yearning for food, she went to the banister outside her room and called down, "What time is supper? I'm starved."

"In an hour or two, I imagine. This bird is tougher than I thought."

Two hours later Ophelia called down again. "Good God, Red. If it's much longer I'm going to eat my pillow."

There was no answer.

"Red? Isn't that swan done yet?"

Still, no answer.

"Red Cane? In another minute I'm coming down there."

Silence. Ophelia slipped into her robe and went down. The dining table was set for two as usual. The baked swan cooled on a platter in the kitchen. But Red was nowhere to be seen. She went into the kitchen and through a pantry window saw a lantern in the potting shed. Red had probably gone to get fresh herbs to garnish the bird or add to the stuffing. Slipping on a pair of galoshes, she lit a candle. The new moon had gone suddenly dark and it was black as pitch outside.

She walked carefully from slippery stone to slippery stone until she got to the potting shed, then blew out the candle. She tried the door and found it locked. Wiping the dirty door-glass, she looked in at Peters, lying on the peat pile with his pants pulled down, fanning his rear with a handful of straw. Red, sitting beside him in Mildred Balls's underwear, combed Peters's coarse hair with a tortoise-shell comb. Peters's cheeks were flushed, his eyes half-closed. When Ophelia entered, the scene seemed all the more lurid for the dim lantern and its flicker.

"I hope you don't take any offense," Red said, "but I've just mated with Peters here."

Peters sat up. "I was quietly potting geraniums when that idiot stepped out of a dark corner and made advances, clumsy, lewd advances, with his big willy sticking out. I tried, but I couldn't resist him."

"Is that true, Red, that he put up resistance?"

"He lies like a rug. He clearly indicated he wanted me to sex him good and sex him hard."

Ophelia saw the pointlessness of going any further with the inquiry. "All is forgiven. Let's move past this."

"I'll serve the swan," Red said.

"Listen to me, Red," Ophelia replied. "Wash yourself carefully before you touch any food."

Peters pulled up his underdrawers, then his mud-caked trousers. "What about me? Don't I get any bird? Who chopped its head off? It was me."

"Don't invite him, Miss."

"You hunk of dirt," Peters shouted, making steps toward a digging fork that leaned against a wall. "I'll gig you like a frog."

"See what I mean, Miss? Coarse and dangerous."

"Come on, Peters," Ophelia said, gesturing toward the house. "I'll be leaving tomorrow. Let's eat together and try to make peace. This is exactly what I feared would happen. This is what Mildred warned me about. Now, both of you, take a bath before dinner."

"Water's being rationed, Miss. I neglected to tell you."

"I already cut back on watering things," Peters added.

Red failed to disguise his delight. "So, I suppose Peters and I will have to be bathing in the same tub, in the same water."

"I suppose so," Ophelia said, lifting her dress for the slippery walk back to the house. "But I'm hoping dinner will be served before ten."

"Oh, it will, Miss."

When the time came to eat, Ophelia could only stomach a few bites of the swan's tough, oily breast. She washed them down with gulps of Jake. "Thanks for the effort, you two. My digestion isn't what it used to be."

"That's infuriating," Red snapped. "After all that work. I'd like to cut your throat with a dull knife."

"Calm down, Red Cane."

"See what I mean," Peters said, "He's just plain crazy."

Red puffed out his cheeks, wept weakly, and spat. "I'm so sorry, so ashamed of these uncontrollable urges. I'm going to hang myself."

"There's a good rope in the shed," Peters said. "I'll get it in the morning."

Ophelia had had enough. "This isn't the time for that kind of whining, or that kind of bickering. Now, you'll try to get along and look after things when I'm gone. Grandmother will be back sooner or later. So will I, proba-bly, and Roe too."

"I love Peters," Red said, "despite all. We kissed a hundred times and mated again in the tub."

"For all I care, you can mate at will and forever. I'm going to bed."

Before sunup the next morning Ophelia's Q-ped rolled toward the estate's arched, brick entrance and was about to turn toward Pisstown proper, when she nearly collided with the postman, who said with a wolfish grin, "Whoa, slow down Ophelia girl. I've got brand new shifting orders for you. Ha, ha, ha!"

With her foot heavy on the brake, she read the orders:

SUBJECT: Order to Relocate

Dear Ms. Balls,

The Reverend requests your presence in the city of Bum Bay by 30-Nov. Report to the Templex there no later than six a.m. on that day. There you will serve in the capacity of an acolyte. Duties include but are not limited to attending to the needs of the Abbot. Additional instructions will be conveyed to you upon your arrival.

Your faithful servant,

Reverend Herman Hooker

The Abbot referred to was Dimitri Machnov, the Russian giant. Once the main attraction of many a road show and carnival, the giant had become a true believer in Hooker's teachings and had been appointed Abbot of the Reverend's Bum Bay Templex, the largest, grandest, most influential in the region.

Ophelia first set eyes on Machnov in the Temple's bath house as he floated from one side of the stagnant pool to the other in a loose-fitting pair of rubber nappies. One of his attendants stepped forward to greet Ophelia. "My name is unimportant and I'm to be your Guide. Isn't he a sight to behold? He weighs nine-o-six, his waist measures ninety-three inches and he stands eight-ten. We fear his death will be caused by a fatty degeneration of the heart, probably very soon. This is why we have resorted to bleeding him."

Another attendant waded into the pool with a bucket of leeches. "These little medical miracles come all the way from the Fertile Crescent." The attendant took leeches from the bucket and placed them at intervals over Machnov's massive body, even tucking a few beneath the nappies. The giant submitted to this with a contented smile.

Ophelia's Guide said, "What I must see are your shifting papers."

She surrendered the relocation order long enough for the Guide to gloss over it. "Welcome to the Templex. You'll have no name to weigh you down here. We're on a strict no-name basis. And, as a new acolyte, you're under a vow of silence. As a Guide, I'm allowed to speak, out of necessity. Say, haven't I heard of Mildred Balls?"

"My grandmother."

"And Jacob, the brewing magnate? The maker of Jake? Your grandfather?"

"Yes, but he squandered most of his inheritance on a dubious scheme to feed the starving millions in the Fertile Crescent. I have scarcely enough to keep the estate from falling down around me. If I'm away too long, it will collapse."

"Your order says nothing about length of stay. I can only presume it will be five years. There are quarters upstairs for acolytes. You'll be an acolyte until you're elevated to attendant, and then to Guide."

"And my duties will include?"

"Arrangements have been made for children to see Machnov tomorrow. At a reception in the refectory he will shake hands with any children who desire to meet him and fill their sacks with roasted nuts and nonpareils. He then will lead the children on a march to Hooker Park. Your duty on this occasion will be to periodically empty Master Machnov's reduction belt, which drains fatty and other secretions through a tube into a bag. You will walk behind him and carry the bag. When it is about three-fourths full, it will be disconnected and emptied into the gutter."

The Guide escorted Ophelia to her quarters, a four-by-eight cubicle in a row of twelve others. A cot, a slop bucket, and a wooden stool were the only furnishings. A gel can and a box of matches sat on a small shelf affixed to the wafer-board wall.

"It goes without saying that if you are heard addressing another attendant or acolyte, you will be punished with the *bastinado*."

"May I ask what that is, the *bastinado*?"

"We club your feet with cudgels until the bones are thoroughly broken and the inner tissue reduced to jelly. It means life on crutches. Around here idle talk is nothing to be trifled with. Another thing, when you are not actively assisting Machnov, you are expected to immerse yourself heart and mind in Hookerite studies. You'll find the library just off the Abbot's bathing pool, three doors into the east wing corridor. Expect, on a monthly basis, to be tested on your knowledge. Failure there means you'll be *chauffeured*. Do you have any questions or concerns?"

"If I'm *chauffeured*, where will I be taken?"

"Nowhere. The word comes from the French, *chauffeur*, 'to warm.' You are made to lie on a pandiculating appliance, barefoot, while a small fire is lit under your feet and fed fuel until the flesh is burned away."

Ophelia was numb, sleepy, not fully attentive. The two-day pedal tram trip had left her exhausted, her muscles sore. "When is bedtime?"

"We shut our eyes at eight, we open them at four. First, slop jars are emptied and ablutions performed, then we breakfast at five. When morning duties are completed, a noon lunch is served in the refectory. As Machnov usually naps every afternoon, we suggest that time be spent in the library. Supper is at six, postprandial meditations until seven, nightly ablutions, then bed."

"The problem is, I'm not a Hookerite. Some mistake has been made."

"Everyone is a Hookerite, Miss Balls, in spirit if not practice." Ophelia was given a copy of the *Field Guide*. "I suggest you begin by boning up on Hooker's Sayings and be able to write them down in the morning."

"All one hundred and one?"

"Yes. Anything further need explaining before you fall silent for the duration of your stay here?"

"No, nothing more."

Ophelia lay in her cot half the night, reading the Sayings over and over by the dim glow of her gel can, hoping at least a few would stick in her mind. After silently repeating them dozens of times, drowsiness overtook her and she fell asleep. Neither the odor of urine salts lofting from her thin mattress, nor the ringing of the Templex bell every hour, disturbed her rest, as it would have under normal circumstances. Many a night she had lain awake at the estate, personifying sleep, angry at it, sometimes cursing it for its failure to overtake her. She imagined Sleep itself sleeping, snoring thunderously, unaware of her pleadings. After these nights, a fog rolled in and out of her mind all day, and she was constipated. Taken together, the two conditions made her peckish and withdrawn.

When the bell sounded at four, Ophelia awoke groggy and listless to a thin cloud of wood smoke drifting near the ceiling. She could hear the movement of other acolytes in the dormitory, coughing, spitting, nose-blowing and defecating into slop jars. One of them called out, "They're building a fire out there. I'm glad I know *my* Sayings."

Ophelia lit her gel can and, as its shadows played across the ceiling, struggled to remember the Sayings. Even after pulling her hair and rapping herself on the head with her knuckles, she could recall only two: "The meek shall not inherit the Earth" and "Nothing is good that ends well." Nor had she any recall of the numbers that went with them.

Already feeling the flames at her feet, she anxiously took her place at a long table in the refectory. A lively chatter had erupted among the acolytes in general defiance of the no-talk rule. One of them tugged at Ophelia's sleeve. "No need to be so glum. Machnov is dead of heart failure. Don't you smell the smoke? They're burning him now. The Templex is closing and we're all being shifted soon, perhaps today. From this strange place, most anything would be an up-shift."

Ophelia's shifting papers, a packet that included a voucher for a low-priced room at the Gons Hotel, were in her hands before sunset, assigning her to duty as an investigator for the Bum Bay Home Guard. She would inherit certain troublesome cases from a soon-to-be-shifted investigator, a Dutchman by the name of van Vliet.

She was on the late-morning pedal tram and on the other side of Bum Bay before noon to occupy van Vliet's office, though he showed no great haste in emptying his desk and leaving. Every item was carefully studied, thought about, and either tossed into the rubbish bin or wrapped in handkerchiefs and carefully packed in an impskin valise.

The Dutchman had a curious bump just above and between his eyebrows, which moved up and down as he talked. "One doesn't want to clean out one's desk in a feverish hurry. You never know what may lie in one of the hidden places behind the drawers."

"Where are they sending you this time?" Ophelia asked.

"To the Purple Isle. I've got a bad case of parasites. If I hold my hand over a candle, you can see them."

"My grandmother is there, in isolation, even with a light load of the little beasts."

"I'm sure they'll isolate me. My load is heavy. They make me fly into rages without warning. I salivate excessively. Sometimes you'll see me with one end of a twisted hankie sitting in my mouth. It wicks down into a sponge I keep in my top pocket. If I'm walking down the street I'll step into an alley periodically and wring it out."

"I wish you the best of luck."

"The same to you, and if I were you, I'd avoid the night watchman. He reports at 9:10. Comes in the back door. He's a goon without a drop of sense and carries an ice pick. You see this lump on my head?"

"I've wondered about it."

"He stuck me with the pick. It put a dent in my skull. A cyst formed." The Dutchman began to salivate. He twisted an already damp handkerchief, tied a knot at one end and tucked it into his cheek. "Needless to say, my sponge is fairly soaked, and badly needs squeezing. This onrush of spittle can be oafish and offensive at social gatherings, on the buses, anywhere."

"My sympathies." Ophelia glanced at the clock that hung inside a steel-mesh cage on the wall. "Doesn't the pedal tram depart at 9:03?"

"Yes, but I'm on the 9:04 express, the one that's always half empty and the pedaling is brutal. Your best bet is the 8:07, the one that goes to Pisstown. It's got a new gear box and a well-oiled drive chain. You can pedal and sleep at the same time. And you rarely see a stinker on that route. You know how shameless they are about refusing to pedal. I don't know why the Reverend lets them get away with it. There should be a law."

"I'm rather anxious to take a look at these cases," Ophelia whispered.

"All right, then. I'm off to the Purple Isle."

"Before you leave, one question. This seems to be the only occupied office on this floor. I haven't seen anyone else. I've walked up and down the hallways. There are hundreds of office spaces, all empty. Except one. There was a bed in 144. A cot, actually."

"That's where the watchman sleeps."

"He isn't much of a watchman, then, if he's asleep."

"It struck me odd as well, but I never questioned him . . . there's a working toilet in 141. The water is turned on for an hour in the morning and an hour at night."

"Thank you so much for all that information."

"You're probably anxious to pursue these cases, but I'll warn you, you'll have little or no capacity to do it at anything but a snail's pace. If you want to interview a subject, it is up to you to make your way to their whereabouts by pedal bus, foot, Q-ped or other means, and at your own expense. You have the authority to compel subjects to travel to your office for interrogation, but you have no way to know their whereabouts either, or to notify them by mail. That, too, will be impossible. There is no stationery, writing instrument or stamps. And who would deliver it anyway? Postal service ended after the Chaos."

"Thank you again. I *am* curious about the cases. I'll do what I can under the restrictions."

The Dutchman lifted a pants-leg and shook out a few drops of urine. "Now look what I've done. I've pissed myself. Damn it to hell. I've got it on my shoe. I'll be laughed off the tram. Oh, well, what can I do? Those are your cases, now, Miss Balls." With a click of his heels and a victory sign, the Dutchman jerked the door open and left, leaving a small puddle behind.

Ophelia decided the puddle would dry of its own accord. She was finally able to sit down and have a look at the cases, to engage her mind in serious matters. The one recorded on the top form detailed the finding of a corpse in the street—"Clothing worn backward, clogs on the wrong feet. It is my thought that she had been dumped from a moving conveyance. A postmortem on the female subject was inconclusive as to cause of death. No identity could be established nor next of kin located. Her body was eventually committed to one of the lime pits at the Stinker Rest landfill."

The next case was that of a Pisstown physician, Dr. Elliott Massengil. The Dutchman had written: "As do certain fungi, Dr. Massengil fed on material already dead, often illegally obtained final-stage stinkers. He stacked them in his barn like cord-wood, drawing canvas cloth over the pile, the summer heat hastening their decomposition. Whenever the doctor vacationed, one of the stinkers went with him in a special-ly-made carpet bag lined with pure, sterile para rubber.

"At some well-defined point in Dr. Massengil's evolution, the line between parasite and predator was crossed. It happened the day his neighbor's wife was found dead. She had been throttled by someone missing a middle finger.

Later, poring over Dr. Massengil's photo album, I was suddenly struck with a furious urgency when a snapshot flopped onto the rug in his home, one of Massengil stripping the trigeminals from a cadaver. His hands were plainly seen. He was missing a middle finger. Here was my man. Case closed."

The watchman appeared at the door of Ophelia's office at 9:10 exactly. He was a pudgy, ill-tempered American with thick cascades of oily black hair.

"Who are you? You must be new. Where's van Vliet? Is he gone to Permanganate already?"

"He left just a few minutes ago."

"You sure?"

"Yes, absolutely."

"He was always pissing in his pants, that thick-headed son of a bitch. I hated him so much I juked him between the eyes with my pick." The watchman displayed the pick lying flat in the palm of his hand. "You his replacement?"

"I'm taking over his cases. They shifted me here."

"I'm Karl, night watchman. They used to call me Cowfoot. I've gone barefoot all my life. Never once had on a shoe. Winter, summer, fall, never a shoe. My feet got awful tough, you know. Now they're numb and cold as the ground they step on."

"I'm Ophelia."

"That's not a Dutch girl's name, is it?"

"No, no. It isn't at all."

The watchman shuffled his way down the hall. "I guess I'll go on down to 144 and catch a short nap." Ophelia saw the ice pick sticking out of his pocket. "I like you," he said. "I can tell you're an honest person. That's why I'm not going to stick you. Soon as I saw the Dutchman, I knew I'd be pulling the pick on him."

Shortly before twelve, when Ophelia was about to leave for the night, she was startled to see someone standing in the office door, a disfigured young woman with a single, blond braid as thick as a ship's rope. Her eyes were crossed, her nostrils widely flared, her lower lip sagged, her gums were blue, her fingers all the same length. Some of her dull, green teeth had small patches of algae growing on them. Ophelia couldn't look her in the eye.

"Is this the Home Guard office?"

"Yes, it is. But we're closed. We've been closed for hours."

The woman drooled, then wiped it away with a wet bandana. "That Dutchman, van Vliet, is he here? I'm looking for that Dutchman."

"I've taken over his cases. He's doing time at Permanganate Island."

"That can't be. I'm supposed to mate with him. We were going to have some babies after I recover from my genital surgery. All the organs come from a donor stinker, but they swore the kids would be normal. They guaranteed it. Who are you?" She drooled again and wiped it away.

"Ophelia, his replacement . . . . It's interesting that you have the same condition he had."

"Yeah, what's that?"

"Excess saliva."

"I always had it, since I was born."

"They say the shifting is random, but I sometimes wonder. The two of you, the same condition."

"What am I supposed to do? They shift me here to mate with this Dutchman, who's got the same saliva problem. I reserve the bridal suite at the Gons, and they send him to Permanganate Island before I get here."

"Let's go see the watchman. Maybe he knows what to do."

The door to 144 was closed, with carpet scraps stuffed under it. Ophelia knocked repeatedly. "Are you in there, Karl? I just wanted to tell you there's someone here by mistake."

She put her ear to the door. "Karl?" She could hear hoarse breathing.

"Don't make me open the door, girl. I've got a bad case of the black twirlies."

"There's someone here. Some kind of mistake. She was supposed to mate with the Dutchman."

"Is she cock-eyed?"

"Yes."

"Off-putting face?"

"Some would think so."

When the carpet pieces were pulled away and the door swung open, there Karl sat, cleaning his ice pick with an oiled cloth.

Ophelia turned to the disfigured girl. "I'd like you to meet Karl, the watchman."

Karl held the pick out of sight behind his back. "Come closer, girl. Let me get a good look."

The girl stepped closer to the watchman, who stood up and examined her face closely. "Ophelia, it looks like we've reeled in a big fish here. She's a carrier. What's your name, girl?"

"Daisy."

"Daisy who?"

"Doolittle." Her voice faltered, her eyes blinked rapidly.

"She carries the parasite. I can tell by that face. And I'll wager she's been spreading it around, infecting hundreds."

"She was shifted here," Ophelia said, "to mate with van Vliet."

"Get her out of the building before I stick her." The watchman disclosed his freshly-oiled pick and placed its sharp point on the girl's breast bone. "You've infested people. And those people have infested other people. I'm almost in the mood to send you off to another world in the name of the Reverend, for better or worse."

Ophelia turned away, thinking she might hear the pick *shhhump* into the girl's chest, but Karl, instead, took a lump of willy from his top pocket and ate it. "All right, Daisy," he said, flinging the pick into the wall, "The old willy just reprieved you." He looked at Ophelia. "Take her out to the alley. The City'll pick her up."

Ophelia grasped the young woman's hard, cold hands and dragged her by fits and starts to the freight door, down the loading-dock steps and into the alley. A pedal truck was parked close by, workers flinging stinkers into the bed.

"She's a carrier," Ophelia said.

"Don't matter. We'll take her anyway. Night, Ma'am."

Two workers lifted the Doolittle girl by her hands and feet and flung her into the bed, where she landed atop a pile of put-down stinkers collected from Bum Bay alleyways.

"You'll all be sorry for this. It's not the last you'll hear from me. My next stop is Pisstown. I'll find the perfect mate."

Out of sympathy, Ophelia waved half-heartedly. "Good luck, Daisy."

His face as red as a berry, Karl was sitting in Ophelia's chair eating a starch bar stuck on the end of his pick when she returned to her office. "Just a warning, kid," he said. "I'm feeling restless, a little explosive. The willy does that sometimes. If you're here much longer I may fall into a rage and stick you twenty or thirty times."

Without a second thought, Ophelia left the building and walked one block to the old hotel. Crumbling with neglect, its awnings were shredded and flapping noisily in an icy wind and there were patches of brown lichen on the brickwork. But inside, a glowing pellet stove kept the lobby warm and the candles of a small café tucked into a corner shone brightly.

Ophelia bought a *City Moon* and sat down to have a late supper there. It wasn't long before she noticed a man in a back booth staring conspicuously at her while he dunked a johnnycake into a bowl of Canal fish stew, then kneaded it like dough with fingers that were thick at the hilts and tapered to small, sharply pointed nails. He then stuffed it down in a fit of clumsy swallowing.

Ophelia ordered the stew and a Jake before opening her *City Moon* to look for news about the Chaos in Pisstown. But the man watched her continuously, coughing, clearing his throat, puckering his lips, blowing her kisses, tapping his tin spoon on the table to get her attention, all the while holding a clove-scented urpflanz cigar clenched in his front teeth. It was impossible for her to concentrate on the news. She turned away from the annoyance and looked out at the street. Workers shuffled wearily along, heads bowed to the wind. The streetlamps were running low on fuel, some completely out. Others crackled and glowed dimly blue.

One of Hooker's Guards came into the café out of the cold. A crust of ice had formed on both his epaulets, just above the obvious bulge of a pistol in a holster abreast of the armpit. After conversing briefly with the rude man in the back booth, during which the subject seemed to be Ophelia, he came to her booth.

"He says you bother him. Are you looking to do some time at Permanganate?"

"I was just reading the newspaper. What have I done to bother him?"

"He wanted to kiss you. You spurned his advances."

"Hasn't he heard? It's against the law. And that isn't the only reason."

"He *has* heard. That's the Reverend himself."

"It *is* him. Now I see. I'm sorry."

The Guard returned to the Reverend's booth for additional consultation, after which he beckoned to Ophelia with a wave of the arm and the Reverend said, "Come on over here, you."

A kiss from the Reverend seemed the better of the choices facing her and she went to his booth.

71

"Let me give you a big juicy smack on those pretty lips, Honey Pie," the Reverend said. "I'll hand you a ticket to the best show in town."

"The Moldenke show," the Guard said.

She leaned over, closed her eyes and waited. After a few moments, the Reverend's dry lips, along with the spiked hairs that surrounded them, passed across hers, then returned, this time with protruding tongue, which he forced into her mouth more than once in rapid succession.

When it was over, she opened her eyes. The Reverend was holding out the ticket. "Here, Honey. Enjoy the show. That Moldenke is something to behold. He and I were friends for a while."

"You'll like the show," the Guard said. "Moldenke says things you'll find hard to believe. He'll play tricks on your mind."

The Reverend stood up to leave. "Excuse me, now, Honey, but my Q-ped is waiting."

"Come with me," the Guard said. "We'll take a pedal cab to the show. It's at the Radiola Theater."

The closer the cab approached the Radiola, the more elusive the theater became in the frozen night-mists that had settled over everything. Without visible landmarks to steer him in the right direction, the stinker cabby circled the same blocks, re-crossed the same intersections over and over again. His apologies and excuses were effusive. "My vision is going. I can see nothing in this fog. You mustn't hate me. I've taken hundreds of fares to the Radiola. I beg you to believe we're getting closer."

"Stop!" the Hookerite said. "Let us out. We'll find it on foot." To Ophelia, he said, "Pay him a buck or two."

Ophelia paid the fare without complaining.

There was no one on the street to ask directions of, but Ophelia eventually spotted the white beam of an arc light searching the sky. "That's the Radiola," the Hookerite said. "It has a searchlight on the roof."

Crossing a soggy, abandoned lot overgrown with urp-flanz, then navigating muddy, unlit alleyways for almost an hour, Ophelia and the Hookerite finally came to the theater. A red arrow under a flickering bulb angled downward, indicating the entrance.

The Hookerite said, "This wasn't always a theater, you know. It was a school, back in the time of Sinatra. Have you heard of schools?"

"I've read about schools in books I have. It's good that we don't need them now. They would be useless, wouldn't they?"

"This one was closed after the first Chaos. It was the wise thing to do. Don't you agree?"

"It seems reasonable."

"Follow me. I've been here before."

Once inside, they were in an ink of darkness. Ophelia followed the Hookerite to reserved seats in the front row as the host took the stage. "Ladies and gents, let's welcome Moldenke to Bum Bay. Call him a stinker, a death traveler, call him what you will, but one thing we know for sure. Moldenke's been gone and come back and all he wants to do is tell us how it is over there."

With a stinker's gait and using a cane, Moldenke took his place center stage. He wore black rags and a wide-brimmed white hat that kept his face in shadow. When he turned his head to assess the size of the audience, Ophelia observed an inch-long tube of flesh protruding from just below his ear. It had the general appearance and shape of an infant's finger, but lacked a nail. In the end of the tube, a small hole leaked a clear, gelatinous fluid. To Ophelia the protuberance looked like some kind of shunt, or drain, not a natural growth, something done surgically.

"I don't recall that the place had a name," Moldenke began. "It may have been illuminated from within, like a lantern-bug. Stars? Moon? I don't know. I never looked up much. We were mostly focused on what was in our own bailiwick. At first I lived in Bailiwick 246. That's not far from Indian Apple, a heavily populated city. There was anywhere from a hundred to a thousand of us, depending. The bailiwick population fluctuated fiercely. Everyone lived in a trailer.

"My neighbors were the Rosenbergs, Ethel and Julius. If we opened our respective doors at the same time, they would bang together. The trailers were side-by-side and front-to-front all the way to the end. If I wanted to go down to the well for a bottle of muddy water, I had to walk sideways about a half mile. It was so narrow a passage that if you met somebody coming the other way, one of you would have to crawl under a trailer till the other one could pass.

"Beyond my bailiwick, there was nothing but wide, open spaces. I guess it was best to live as near the well as possible. This one wasn't a very good one, though. The water was foamy and mud-flecked, but it satisfied thirst enough and didn't rot your teeth like some of the waters in some of the bailiwicks.

"That's what would start a bailiwick, drilling down and getting water from anything you could tap into. Sometimes old swimming pools underneath would have water in them. But it tasted like bile. And sometimes, little pieces of bone might get sucked up in the pump and land in your sink. Somebody would get lucky and tap into a frozen-over reservoir. And that bailiwick might last a few years, maybe a hundred. Some of them, they would go dry in six months. Or they would drill into a big cesspool and get nothing but a gush of sewer water, mixed with alkali and radium. So, when somebody drilled a good, clean well, the trailers would come.

"Holly Island had a lot of bailiwicks because of all the swimming pools down below to tap into. That's also where they were digging up frozen heads. It seemed that anyplace where there were a lot of swimming pools, you'd find a lot of frozen heads. The surface soil on Holly Island was soft and dark, mostly rotted cloth, straw, old ground-up bones and worm castings. It looked rich, like the best soil you've ever seen, and it was loaded with worms, but nothing would grow in it except urpflanz, brambles, touch-me-nots, and camphor bushes.

"When the water source went dry and it was time to go look for another one, we all got together and helped one another move our trailers. We moved in three groups, one behind another, like a train, the ones in front pulling, the ones in back pushing. It was hard work and it took forever. But what are you going to do when the well runs dry? We did try to train boar hogs to pull the trailers, but that was a failure. No matter how many of them you hitched up, you couldn't get any organized pull out of them. It was pandemonium. We gave up on that project.

"Later on I stayed in Bailiwick 212, which formed over an old hand-dug well fed by a natural spring, which was a lucky find. It was where the old town of Harpstring had been. That was before the Chaos I think. It was just some old wooden buildings where some early stinkers lived. They told me the Harpstringers used to grow grain and eat big pancakes. Then came the hundred year drought. Nobody could farm anything. If they could raise any grain at all, the grasshoppers would eat it. So the hardy Harpstringers ate grasshoppers. They roasted them, boiled them, ate them raw and pickled them."

Here Moldenke, seemingly disoriented, took a sudden step backward and fell squarely on his head. He lay there a minute, with no one in the audience offering help, then sat up. When he removed his hat it was easy to see that the back of his head had been crushed when it hit the stage floor, yet there was no blood, nor did he show signs of distress or pain.

The host took the stage. "That's all, folks. That's the show for tonight." He lifted Moldenke's feet in his hands and dragged him off the stage.

At the same time, a small company of Hookerite Guards went up and down the aisles, holding gel cans in front of certain faces and looking closely at them. When the can was held in front of Ophelia's, one of the Guards said, "Ophelia Balls?"

"Yes."

"It looks like some strings have been pulled, Miss Balls, by your grandmother. I hear she's being released from Permanganate. You're being sent home."

The news parted Ophelia's lips in a broad smile as two Guards escorted her out of the Radiola, one holding onto each of her elbows.

As she waited for the 9:30 to Pisstown, delighted to be going home, she saw the Reverend blow her a kiss and wave as his pedal car passed by.

Five.

William Parker Yockey, adolescent leader of the Hookerites, wants the goods and assets of final-stage stinkers distributed among the less fortunate. It's an old idea with a new twist. Needs are few for stinkers reaching the fourth stage. All the senses dulled, no hunger, no thirst, limited excretory functions. To build remote encampments, where stinkers would simply wait, would not be a costly proposition, say the Hookerites.

Yockey was interviewed the day he turned twelve. He was ensconced in his little Canal-side shanty on Coggshell Avenue, really nothing more than a lean-to made of crate-wood, but spacious and weather-tight.

He said, "What is a flag, after all? Is it not something like a curtain? On one side of it stand the wealthy and privileged, on the other the rest of us. I have a pile of flags outside the back door. I burn them in my stove when fall-wood is scarce." Here he went out and came back with an armload of flags. "They have so many pigments," he said, "the flames dance colorfully behind the mica windows of the fire door, entrancing me of a winter's night. You might say I am warmed by the heat of national fervor."

As the interview progressed, Yockey drank Jake, smoked an urpflanz pipe and fed flag after flag to the fire. When pressed for details of future plans for his party, he said, "In the next election the Reverend will run and win on a simple idea, that stinkers must be isolated from the rest of us. In a few months we can build ten or twenty camps. Think of it this way—eventually everyone dies, even stinkers, although they take a while longer on average. Hooker says, 'Let's put them out of the way once and for all. They can wait in peace and quiet. They can listen to the chirp of sparrows, the croak of frogs, the hum of the bee. Not a worry in the world.'"

Some of the Reverend's Guards are puzzled over an imp keeping a vigil beside an old black shoe. The imp, apparently an abandoned pet, refuses to go farther than fifteen feet from the well-worn size twelve even to eat, a Guard said yesterday, who first noticed the loyal watch-keeping last week. By day the critter stays close to the shoe, now invaded by mold and beetles, along a wooded section of the Canal. At night it curls next to the shoe and goes to sleep whining. "The only time it gets upset is if someone picks up the shoe," one Guard said.

It comes to me from good authority that property on Square Island is being appropriated by the Administration. Why? Well, the Reverend wants to sink a huge tooth-gold mine there. It seems preliminary tests have indicated a massive concentration of stinker remains about sixty feet down. It's hard to differ with the Reverend's view when you consider that he has sole ownership of the only steam shovel on the Island and the only mules to move it.

Once mules were a common sight on any street in Pisstown, until the first great Chaos, when they were slaughtered and canned to feed a meat-starved populace. The cans were labeled "Ideal Food For You," the inference being that you were able to consume this meat with no injurious effects. Historical accounts, however, tell us differently. The meat smelled putrid and was often wormy.

Roe's shifting orders directed him to travel to a specified address in central Bum Bay, where he would mate with someone by the name of Daisy Doolittle. When he stepped off the pedal tram, a bank of low thunderheads filtered the fading sunlight in such a way that its rays presented a stunning system of converging bars of shadow against the eastern sky. In the wavering light, he was having trouble reading street signs.

A friendly American who saw him looking around in every direction stopped to help. "Let me guess, you've been shifted here to mate with Daisy Doolittle. You want to know where she is and where the line is forming, don't you?"

"I have her address."

"My name's Frank Johnson. I know where she is. We all know. You play the saw, I see. That's got entertainment value. Makes you worth something."

"I'm Roe Balls. Grandmother says I'm a prodigy. Grandfather says I'm a savant." After a deep cough, he had a swallow of the sour-tasting cough medicine Ophelia had concocted. "This is my first shift and my first mating. I'm anxious."

"Daisy's a hard one to mate with. They say there's only one male out here with the key that'll unlock her, if you get my meaning. No other one will fit right. She'll kick you six feet in the air. She's strong as a mule."

"How do I get to this address?"

"Come with me. It's the old Radiola Theater, over in the Heritage Area. People get side-shifted there, like me, like you. Some bug got in the system. Everybody thinks they're here to mate with the Doolittle girl. *Ha.* We're here to sit around in a broken-down old movie house and wait for the next shift."

"How long?"

"Nobody knows. Whenever the Reverend declares another round of shifting."

Roe followed the fast-paced American, always a few strides behind, until they came to the unlighted dark side. In windows gel cans burned dimly. Street lamps flickered. "From here on," the American said, "power comes and goes unpredictably. This part of town awaits the wrecking ball. As far as Hooker is concerned, it's already a pile of rubble. Whatever works, whatever runs, it's thanks to us, not the Reverend."

When Roe and the American arrived tired and sweaty at the Radiola, other side-shifted settlers waited in line at a glass-enclosed ticket window. The power had come on in the neighborhood and the theater was brightly lit. Above them, a marquee's sagging letters read "Miracle in the Grotto."

"They check new people in here," the American said. "This place used to be a school. Then it was a movie house. Now it's a waiting area. Get in line. I'll meet you at the candy counter."

"Thank you for all the help. I would have been lost."

"No problem. I'm a Johnson. We help out."

Roe reached into his bag. "Let me give you a few bucks."

"We don't expect anything in return, either. See you at the candy counter."

To amuse himself as the line slowly edged forward, Roe took out his saw and prepared to play. Normally, when he played, he sat. This time there was no place to sit, so he stood. With the saw's teeth facing away, he lodged the rag-wrapped handle against his shoulder, placing his left thumb on the blunt tip of the blade and his left fingers on the other side. He pressed down to form a slight "S" curve in the metal and began stroking with his bow. After three strokes, the saw began to sing. The men in line were livened and entranced.

"I never heard a saw played like that," one of them said. "That's far above an octave and a half." Another balled up a buck note and threw it at Roe's feet. Quickly other notes were tossed his way and applause erupted. "You should put out a hat. You could make a living," someone shouted. "Can you play 'Red River Valley'?"

Roe played that song, one tone flowing smoothly into the next as he bent the blade back and forth, then "Moonlight on the Wabash" and "My Old Kentucky Home." His bouncing foot produced a vibrato.

He continued playing as the line shortened until he reached the window, when an official inside, raising one eyebrow, spoke through a perforated metal plate in the ticket-booth glass. "Let's see those shifting orders."

Roe produced the form from his upper pocket and slid it through a portal in the glass.

"Balls. That name strikes a bell. Why?"

"I don't know," Roe said.

"I know. Your grandfather was the late Jacob Balls. I'm surprised his widow didn't use her civic influence to get you out of the shifting process."

"She's at Permanganate Island. Out of touch."

"That's a shame. Half the world is going there." The official went over the papers again. "And you were shifted here to mate with the Doolittle girl, like most of these other poor suckers? I hate to tell you, but there's a long line ahead of you."

"I don't understand."

"We're sorry about the snafu, but what the heck, complex systems go haywire. It's all part of Hooker's grand scheme, which allows plenty of room for failure along the way. Go inside, find yourself a seat, start the waiting process."

Shortly after, Roe came to the candy counter and waited for the American. Beneath the cracked glass case, moths flew about over candy bars ridden with white maggots. At the end of the counter a popcorn machine still held the last batch of corn popped, now brown and moldy and seething with ants.

The American showed up, yawning. "I fell asleep. I hope you didn't wait long. Come on, I saved you a seat." Roe followed him into the seating area. Of the hundred or so seats, more than ninety were occupied. "If you don't get a seat you could be standing for a long, long time." They found the seats and settled into them. "These are good ones. The springs haven't popped through."

"What do we do now, Frank?" Roe asked.

The American chuckled. "Nothing. We sit here and wait. The power's on. That's good. When that happens they show a movie. Otherwise we sit in the dark or light candles if you can find one. Matches are scarce, too."

"I'm hungry," Roe complained.

"Don't worry. They'll pass out some starch bars and some willy. Here they come now."

Barefoot stinkers in ushers' uniforms pushed wheelbarrows up the aisles, distributing starch bars, low-grade willy, and bottles of Jake. The hand-size starch bars were wrapped in wax-soaked paper and could be eaten in two or three bites. The willy was in pellet form, the Jake diluted, its normal yellow hue almost absent.

Roe gobbled down his starch bar and followed it with a slosh of Jake and the lump of willy. "Not so bad," he said.

"You should have saved your willy for later," the American advised. "You'd sleep better."

The shabby curtains opened and the movie began. The American sighed, "I've seen this a thousand times."

The film began with a scene in which Hooker, dressed in winter clothes, approaches the dark entrance of The Grotto, a restaurant conducting business inside a shallow cave. The host, a stinker, is there to greet him: "Honored sir, Pliny referred to this grotto as the breathing place of Pluto, where the fiends of the infernal regions found ventilation and fresh air when Hades became too hot for comfort. Therefore, you might imagine the air to be naturally cool. That is not true. You see, a warm carbonic gas percolates through the floor.

The place is uncomfortably warm to anyone who is not a fiend. But I must caution you, the gas can be insidious if you breathe it for long. That's why we limit diners to twenty-five minutes, even very important people, and why we close for the summer."

The Reverend places his hand on top of the host's head. "Loosen up, you stiff!" In close-up, viewers see the stinker's gray cheeks redden, his eyes light up, his dry, spongy lips fill with moisture.

The Radiola's power failed, the film stopped, and the theater darkened.

Beset suddenly with a fit of coughing, the American lit a candle, saying it was his last. When he caught his breath he said, "The air in here is bad for the lungs. Falling plaster dust is what it is."

Roe gave his bottle of cough syrup to the American, who held it well above his open mouth and poured in a dram or two. "Mmmmmmm. That's righteous good."

A few industrious stinkers moved up and down the aisles selling hand-made tallow candles and matches whose tips were dipped in poor quality sulfur and excessive amounts of phosphorous. Small flaming chunks often flew from the tips when they were struck, sometimes setting the user's clothing on fire or landing in an eye. "Candles here. Candles and matches. What'll you give me?"

Gel cans were lit and placed along the edge of the stage. An usher spoke through a bullhorn. "All right, everyone. Keep the chit-chat to a minimum. If any of you want to come down and entertain, please do. Curfew in one hour."

A stinker sitting behind Roe thumped him on the head and said, "Go down on that stage and play your saw. I heard you out there. You're terrific. Put out a hat. You'll make a killing."

Roe went to the stage and played on for more than an hour. His prodigious skills kept listeners attentive and quiet.

He took modest bows between pieces and the flicker of the gel cans lent the evening a small degree of graciousness. Bucks were balled up and thrown to the stage, at which point a well-dressed gentleman in a silk suit and impskin boots made an appearance onstage.

"Jerry Grandee. Let me manage you, sonny boy. You'll make me rich. I'll make you happy. You play the saw like an angel. Can you dance?"

"No."

"I'm always on the lookout for young men with your talents. Can you sing?"

"Only the Edelweiss song. My sister taught it to me."

"Not such a problem. I'm Ray. Ray Harp."

"Didn't you say you were Jerry . . . ?"

"Did I say I was Jerry, Jerry Grandee?"

"You did."

"Sorry. A little white lie. It's nothing. My tongue slipped. Look, the truth is, I run a private club called The Bones Jangle. Very hush-hush. It's in the basement. I book acts. We serve a limited clientele, you understand. Everything's extremely sub rosa. Come on down. I'll show you the place. We'll talk turkey."

"I want to bring my friend, Frank."

"Can't do that. I know Frank. He's a reprobate, a petty thief, and a congenital liar. Not allowed in the club."

"That's a shame."

Down a steep set of stairs, the Bones Jangle door stood slightly ajar and the sweet odor of burning urpflanz drifted out. Roe heard excited conversation, annoyingly loud once he was inside. At the far end of a long, narrow space, on a raised platform, a human skeleton hung on a stand. Bathed in a dim red light from a spot above and powered by some unseen mechanism, it danced a jig. The syncopated jangle of its bones provided lively ambient sound. Down the center of the space was a series of eight raised platforms with round tables atop them, each with four sets of pedals. New arrivals sat drinking Jake as they pedaled and chatted.

Grandee sat Roe down at the table nearest the skeleton. "Here's a good spot. The show will start in a few minutes." He flagged down a server. "Two Jakes for me and my client here."

Roe strapped his feet to the pedals.

"It keeps the power on," Grandee said, "for the stage lights, for Mr. Bones Jangle over there, for the icebox."

"You want me to play my saw?"

"I do, but not tonight. The Doolittle girl's on for tonight. She's in big demand, a showpiece. It was a tough negotiation with her family, but she's mine now. They'll wheel her out in a minute."

"That's what my shifting order said. That I was going to try to mate with Daisy Doolittle."

"That's what they told all those dopes upstairs. But here's a little secret between you and me. There's very few sets of gonads that'll work with what she's got. One could be yours. If it is, you'll be upshifted for certain. You want to give it a try sometime? I'll put you on the list."

"I've never mated before."

"Don't worry. She'll tell you what to do when the time comes. Go, get in line."

A server brought the Jake as a queue of young male shiftees formed at the edge of the platform.

Grandee finished off his Jake in two swift gulps as the nude Doolittle girl was lifted to the platform and placed on a pandiculating appliance. "The show's about to start. Pedal harder. Keep the lights bright."

At that moment, a squad of Guards entered The Bones Jangle and put a halt to everything. "Stop pedaling and remain in your seats!" The clatter of the pedal chains diminished, Mr. Bones Jangle ceased his dance and the room darkened. One of the Guards removed his tunic and covered the Doolittle girl with it. "We'll be taking names now," he said. "You'll all be going to work on the Reverend's imp farm for a while."

"Just when I had a going thing happening here," Grandee sighed.

"I do like the out-of-doors," Roe said.

Six.

Life is cheap in Pisstown's Heritage Area, where a second-stage stinker named Hot Rod Lush packs a triple threat. It is a place where kinsmen murder kinsmen, robbers murder merchants, wives murder husbands, husbands slay wives, cousins murder cousins, sons kill fathers, sweethearts erase sweethearts and friends, friends. The great variety of homicides in that part of the city has provoked the Reverend and his Guards, but not soon enough to stop Hot Rod Lush. He and his brother, Calvin Lush, argued over their younger brother being arrested for unlawful sexual congress with a young male stinker. One said he believed he was guilty, the other said no. This produced a snappy death in blazing gunsmoke from an antique .38 caliber pistol. Boom! Hot Rod, in his fury, had gone to Calvin's Q-ped and gotten the weapon. He'd swept it in front of Calvin's face and said, "What the hell did you say? I'll mow you down," and poured a bullet into Calvin's head. Another life was gone from the Heritage Area, another sad funeral arranged.

Muffy Brown, a twenty-three year old stinker, has spent the last nine years blowing herself up. In that time she has used more than a van load of dynamite to send herself whirling through over eight hundred explosions. Muffy is the feature attraction of the Reverend Hooker's Stunt Show, which travels city to city and town to town. Twice each performing day, she puts what's left of her life on the line with nine *sticks of dynamite. She sits in yoga fashion, her head tucked between her legs, in the center of a three-sided, tin-covered capsule. The countdown begins. At zero, she lights the main fuse with a match. Then, a terrific explosion sends her flying out of the capsule. For fifteen minutes following the explosion, Muffy writhes on the ground, not knowing where she is. The explosion has knocked the air out of her lungs and, like a drowning person, she must be forced to breathe again. Three men are assigned to see that she is revived.*

A man was saved from a chilly drowning yesterday by the Reverend's brother, Wallace "Buddy" Hooker, who has volunteered for duty with the life-saving crew organized by the Health Department at the Disinfecting Station at 10th and Flum. As chief frogman of the crew Buddy was there on the dock about six o'clock in his rubber frog feet and bathing suit, when he saw a man floating down the Canal like a log and calling for help. Buddy dove into the disinfected downstream water and swam out to the man, who threw his arms around Buddy's neck and gave him a hard battle. The man, attempting to escape from Permanganate Island, had floated across the Straits, a distance of sixty miles, then swam into the mouth of the backward-flowing National Canal another five miles before being snatched out of the rushing current and swiftly returned to the Purple Isle.

Buoyed by all the publicity, Wallace has put his energies and his brother's influence into organizing Frogmen for Hooker, already boasting ten thousand members and growing. Those joining get a miniature pair of frog feet for attaching to a key chain, to wear in a lapel, or hang in a window as a lucky charm. In addition they get a free copy of the Reverend's Field Guide.

Unable to find employment after his release from Permanganate Island, a Pisstown stinker, whose identity is unknown, wandered aimlessly from one place to another, blown about like a leaf in the wind. Having landed in Witchy Toe one cold day, he was taken into custody and placed in the lockup where he had access to the stove. That night he heated the poker red hot, placed the end against the wall and threw himself against the point. The instrument plowed its way into his abdomen, searing the parts entered. Another wayfarer occupying the cell with him was asleep when the drastic action took place, so it is not known how long the stinker survived.

A strange creature of the deep beached itself on Square Island a little over a year ago. Nearly seven feet long, with a high, flattened body, tall fins, a three-tentacled mouth encircled with sharp teeth and a "chopped-off" appearance, the specimen has been called a hagfish. Held in captivity for study, it has demonstrated the ability to breathe through its eyes, see through its skin and tie itself into knots. It can live without food for more than a year and when it is afraid it hides in a globule of jelly-like material secreted into the surrounding water. The creature has five hearts, each beating in a different rhythm, and each controlling separately the head, tail, tentacles, muscles and liver. Fearing there may be more of these things in the waters around the Island, authorities have urged people not to wade in the shallows, where one of them may be watching for feet, or to dawdle long enough for a bite to be taken and blood sucked from a tender calf or ankle.

It was little reported in the press, but Reverend Hooker recently had a narrow escape from death. The well-known aviator, Peter Knabenshue, nearly took off the Reverend's head when the screws of his orbigator suddenly spiraled downward in the vortex of a whirling wind. As Knabenshue lost control of the aircraft, it took a dangerous tilt to one side and swooped over the crowd, plucking off the Reverend's hat.

William Parker Yockey, adolescent Hookerite leader, was out campaigning for the Reverend yesterday. He told an audience at Pisstown, "As the Reverend has said many times, the shifting policies are intended to stimulate business and at the same time achieve long-term prosperity, fiscal and personal. It's a beautiful concept. You may be moved down the street or across the Bum Bay Straits. Think of it also as a cure for boredom, a way to perk up the citizenry, a way to give the people new energies, new jobs, new children and spouses. Sure, some will win, some will lose. You'll have up- and down-shifts, you'll have side-shifts too. And in five years, another round of shifting will come along."

He was asked how long it would be before someone tampers with the process and arranges self-advantageous shiftings? Yockey's answer: "The tide of social change will rise so rapidly that such persons will drown, their voices hushed."

And what does side-shifting entail? Yockey says, "These individuals may find themselves in a kind of social limbo for a while, out of the game as it were. They may undergo long periods of waiting, but isn't waiting good for the soul? Isn't it what life is all about?"

And with all the intermixing that comes along with the shiftings, he was asked, "What about the spread of parasites?" Yockey had a ready answer for that, too: "It will serve to weaken the parasites by spreading them thinly."

At home again and in charge of the family estate, Ophelia was in a funk much of the time. There were hundreds of things to do. Caring for the kitchen drain alone was a time-consuming occupation. A drain could kill, she knew, and so treated it with respect. She washed it with scalding water and lye soap, poured cupfuls of caustic soda down it every day and at night treated it with chloride of lime. None of this, however, reduced the strength of the cadaverous stink that persisted in rising from it, along with the sound of digging.

"There's a stinker down there," she told the yard man. "I'd like you to get busy and dig him up. We'll take him to the Rest Home."

"I don't want any part of that business," the yard man said, fussy after being awakened from a nap atop a peat pile in the potting shed. "I told your grandmother, I said, 'If a stiff comes up on this property, I'll play no part in getting rid of it.' When that happens, it's time to call in a professional disposal service. I suggest you do the same."

Rather than hire a service and squander the money her grandmother had left behind for maintenance, Ophelia took a shovel and pick and began excavating beneath the main house into the mystery tunnels. After pushing through the first dark, narrow passages, her further investigation disclosed branching, hand-dug tunnels, leading nowhere. She crawled into one of them, thinking she heard digging, and found the stinker she suspected was there.

Startled by Ophelia's candlelight, the stinker dropped his worn spade. "Look at me," he said. "I'm exhausted, dirt-covered, half naked, half dead, and I'm just digging these blind tunnels."

Ophelia pinched her nostrils closed and tried to speak in a calm voice. "You come out with me. I'll have my servant clean you up and fit you with some of my old clothes. You'll be sent to the Rest Home. They'll take care of you there very humanely."

"You don't like my smell, do you?"

"That's right, I don't, but I understand how difficult the stinker life can be. When you get to the Rest Home, your needs will be taken care of. I'm trying to be nice to you. I've been listening to the *chunk-scrape, chunk-scrape* of your shovel for months and listening to the cook complain about the stink making the draperies smell."

"You got any urpmilk?" the stinker asked.

"Sorry, no."

"All right, then. Another time I came up in Istanbul. The Turks packed me in resin, wrapped me in cloth and sent me by canal boat to the demarcation port on the other side of the Bosporus."

"I respect them for that. You do have your sympathizers. Now, for the last time, come out with me. You need to get to the Rest Home. We can't properly care for you here."

"What time is it? Is the sun up or down? I don't like to go up in the bright of day."

"Don't be afraid. The sun is going down."

Persuaded finally by the promise of an outdoor hose-bath, the stinker hobbled into the evening light. "Get me a walking stick before I fall."

Ophelia found a broken rake handle in the potting shed. The yard man, squatting in a corner and moving his bowels into a slop bucket, said, "Good God, that thing stinks."

"I'm going to hose it off and pedal it over to the Home."

"Not soon enough," the yard man said, wiping himself with a handful of peat.

When Ophelia hosed the stinker off, the few pieces of rotted clothing that were intact washed away.

The butler said, "I'll get some hand-me-downs and help the poor creature put them on."

"Please get my Q-ped out of the garage."

"Yes, as soon as I can."

Ophelia struggled to make eye contact with the stinker, who kept turning away. "You're the third one we've dug up this year," she said. "Do you have a name?"

"I forget. Chuck, maybe."

The stinker leaned against the potting shed and continued his laments as Ophelia clipped his long fingernails with the yard man's pruning shears. "After floating up under the Great Salt Lake I was nearly cooked in the hot, stagnant water. Everything tastes salty now."

"You don't say."

"Then there was my coming up in the Heritage Area, so depressed all I did was lie in the gutter like a log of driftwood.

People spit on me. In the mornings, if I felt enough hope, I'd go over to the Red Cross kitchen and get some urpmilk, then go right on back to my gutter. If it rained, I floated down the street. Later, in Pisstown, I built myself a cart and sold toilet goods. I would roll the *City Moon* into a cone and call out to pedestrians, 'I got petroleum jelly, I got witch hazel, Pearly Pink tooth powder, floating soap, talcum by the pound. I got it all.' Then, when I came up in Bum Bay, I always shopped at the Hookerite Market on Gravesend Avenue. I was on a pedal bus going there one day when I was bitten by an enraged American. 'You stiff! You stiff!' he screamed, then stepped on my foot, injuring my plantar wart. Not finished yet, he pounced on me and bit me in the face. I tell you, the punctures almost drained what's left of my life away."

"Why do you go on and on like that? None of it is of any real interest to me."

"All those years of frosty discomfort, alone, trying to dig our way out. We like companionship. We like camaraderie once we find it."

"You'll find that at the Rest Home, I'm sure."

"Will they have urpmilk there?"

"It's very likely."

"That's good. That's good."

Red rolled the Q-ped out of the garage. "Here it is, Miss. I've oiled the chains and greased the sprockets."

"All right, Chuck," Ophelia said, "You look more presentable. Let's get you to the Home."

As Ophelia pedaled out of the estate grounds and toward the Home, the stinker's bare, tattered feet went round and round with the pedals, but the legs were too weak to contribute much to the effort. "Thank you, Miss. It's good to be up on the surface, walking my body around again."

Just ahead the Rest Home was the picture of warmth and comfort. Gel cans burned in every window, Hookerite Sisters of Charity waited at the curb in starched whites to greet new arrivals.

Ophelia patted the stinker on the shoulder. "The Sisters will take good care of you." She stopped pedaling and let the car coast to a stop. "Here we are. There's the Home."

One of the Sisters approached the car carrying a tall glass of urpmilk. She unstrapped the stinker's feet from the pedals and helped him out of the car. "Here you are, my friend. Have a drink before we go in and get you situated."

"He came up under my house, Sister," Ophelia said. "His name is Chuck, he thinks."

"It's quite an act of kindness to bring him here. We'll look after him as long as we can."

"And then?"

The Sister whispered, "He'll be put down humanely."

The stinker drank the urpmilk in a few eager gulps. "Oh, that was good."

"Goodbye, Chuck," Ophelia said. "I'll come and visit."

"Remind me to tell you about the time I came up under the Indiana prairie in the middle of a grasshopper plague. The crops were ruined. All the animals were eaten. It was the worst famine you ever saw."

"I will. I look forward to hearing that."

Ophelia watched him being escorted safely into the Home, then applied her aching legs to the short but uphill pedal back to the estate. When she arrived, both the butler and the yard man were waiting at the entry gate with fresh news.

"I was in the persimmon orchard today," the yard man reported. "I could hear digging. There's another one coming up there. I'm afraid there's one under the breezeway, too."

Ophelia went inside and fixed herself a bowl of urpmeal while Red lit the pellet stove in her bedroom.

"I'm going to sleep late in the morning," she instructed as she spooned the last of her urpmeal from the bowl. "Plan on a late breakfast. After that, I suppose we have some digging to do."

"Yes, Miss, as you say."

"Have Peters lay out picks and shovels, galoshes, and pairs of gloves."

"Yes'm."

"We'll start with the one in the orchard."

Seven.

A neighborhood in Bum Bay lay in awe and wonderment yesterday until the hagfish, which had gushed from a storm drain with a burst of water, had spent its force and crumbled into the gutter. The yellow, sulfurous mist, which came in plumes from its mouth, condensed above the startled onlookers and the sun beat down through it with multiplied ferocity.

In yet another hagfish incident, a worker was hauling a dead one in the bed of his van, strapped, he thought, securely, encircled by rings of inch-thick iron cable. But it rolled off at a narrow turn and hit the pavement in such a manner as to break open and release the same choking, sulfurous gas. Three are dead, including the worker and two bystanders.

Moldenke, the touring stinker, has filed a deed to purchase certain properties in the afterworld. Local legals say the properties do not exist. Moldenke says they do, at the edge of the city, and that he has seen them as recently as two nights ago. "They are vast. Their earth is black, rich and fecund," he told the City Moon. *"It has arable soil, surprisingly rich in nutrients. A white cabbage grows there in profusion." With a wink to one of the Guards, the wig asked Moldenke, "This afterworld of yours. Do the wicked on Earth continue in their wickedness there, and the good in their goodness?"*

Moldenke's answer: "Yes, in churches and nice homes. The wicked get worse, the good go bad, only the indifferent remain the same. The average Joe can't understand it."

He went on to detail his inaugural other-world astonishments: "The first morning I awoke feeling more rested than I had in years. My first surprise was that there wasn't enough fire there to roast an imp. It seemed to have burned out long ago, and a cool drizzle has since turned everything into a slimy, black tar. I saw familiar faces, old friends, generations in single file, squeezed along in a narrow passageway. There are no children there, no animals, an absence of clouds, no urpflanz, the sun is very dim, the nights long, dazzling and bright."

Asked when he first had intimations of the afterworld, he said it had started with a talent show, when he offered his belly to all comers for punching and for charity. Five hundred contestants stood in line for the opportunity. He laughed through the first 1,000 punches, complained of a bellyache at 1,500, spat blood at 2,908 and at 3,000 had to be taken to the Templex clinic, where he "passed away" with a burst abdominal cyst.

He told the paper, "They said I was dead all night long, then I woke up in the morning. No one has offered me a proper explanation yet. That's when I first saw the afterworld, when I 'passed away.' When I woke up, I kept all the memories of the place. It's a real place. I intend to build a retirement home on the land once I find a court to recognize my deed."

Everyone knows the old saying about a snake in the grass. Only a few weeks ago the Reverend stopped to visit his brother, Wallace. They had a very pleasant chat on the patio. Wallace explained his method of brewing "desert" tea, which had none of the tannic bitterness of tea brewed in tin pots, then announced that it was his day to cut the lawn and suggested the Reverend pass the time with a booklet called "Ice Yachts of the Future" while he finished the task.

After a short time, the slashing sound of a sickle was drowned out by the younger Hooker's cry, "I'm bitten! I'm bitten!" It seems that poison from the fangs of a copperhead adder, hiding in the grass, might possibly end Wallace's peripatetic career. What happened was, his sickle struck a stone and fell from his grip. As he reached into the grass to remove it, the snake struck at him, getting its fangs into his hand. In a later release to the press, the Reverend is quoted as saying, "Some degree of mental function has been lost, but Wallace will live. His coma lasted only a few hours. Now he's sitting up and taking hot liquids."

Hookerites have become a law unto themselves. They load their canal boats with Jake and float downstream, bailiwick to bailiwick. At each port they are spoiled with handsome pies baked by admirers and fellow travelers. These houseboat dwellers are not stifled by convention or limitation of any sort. They lie nude in the sun atop their boats if they wish and pass their money ashore for anything they want, with no barriers. Their lives are utterly without responsibility and their lawless practices have caused them to be dreaded by shore people and other boatmen. When they are not stealing, eating, drinking or sleeping, their time is spent playing liar's dice or cut-throat euchre. Bloody quarrels are frequent during these games and sometimes a murder is hidden by the waters of a muddy canal. Fortunately, many Hookerite boats are run down by steamers in the night, owing to the entire crew being asleep or drunk and no light being shone.

At the Reverend's imp farm, Roe served as a lookout, quartered in a watch-tower so high that, had it not lain beyond a curtain of persistent haze, he would have been able to see the wavering glow of Bum Bay. A wooden cistern atop the living quarters collected rain when it came, generally in stingy amounts. The water that dribbled from the faucet was tinted green and had a faintly noxious odor.

With so much time on his hands, Roe was able to play his saw for long hours and still keep an effective eye on the Reverend's imps, who roamed freely over a vast area of damp willow thickets, open meadows of vetch, mallow and wild berries. They were a breed of manipulated imps with the capacity to re-grow muscle. In his "welcome to the farm" speech, the Reverend had told the new arrivals, "Think of it. Just imagine it. Ham, rump roasts, tenderloin, chitterlings, all for the taking, with no pain or discomfort to the imp. In a few days, the meat's all grown back. What could be more providential?"

Roe was told to watch for poachers, who had been seen among the herds with cleavers and wheelbarrows. They were an off-breed band of third-stage stinkers, different in appearance than others. The first time Roe looked, he spotted them in his binoculars. They were short, flat-headed, muscle-bound, and had hard, white skin that shed flakes. If one of them stood still long enough, falling flakes would pile up like snow. There were about ten of them, working as a team. They would encircle the altered imps, tie their legs and cleave as much meat as their wheelbarrows would hold.

While playing a tune on his saw a few foggy mornings later, Roe was thinking he needed to oil the blade to stop it from rusting, when the first poacher to approach the tower did so in a little handmade pedal car with rusted tin can headlamps and a painted-on grill. It was a mystery how he wasn't stung to death by the wasps in the sumac along the ditch-bank.

"You up there. What's that sound? It grates on the nerves. I've been hearing it for miles. It makes me sicker than I am. What do you hope to gain by doing it? Those imps aren't providing the way they were before you moved in here and started your assault on the peace and quiet we like around here."

Roe stepped out onto the rickety metal gallery that surrounded his quarters. "This is as far as you can go," he shouted down. "The limit of the Reverend's property is right where you're parked. Do not proceed an inch farther."

"Let me come up and talk."

"I don't have that authority."

"It doesn't matter. I have it." The poacher held up a sheet of paper. "It's a letter of introduction from the Reverend. Let me come up. This is urgent business."

"All right. I'll read the letter at least. It's a long, hard climb, especially for a short-legged individual like you."

"Best to start right away, then. Promise you won't play that saw while I'm around? My ears are ringing."

"I won't play. It's two hundred and thirty three tall steps. Some of them are loose. Be careful."

Roe opened the door slowly when the out-of-breath little poacher appeared on the gallery.

"Come in. It's chilly out there. I'll make a fire."

The poacher entered warily. Gasping for breath, he looked at Roe's feet with muddy yellow eyes, said nothing, made no gesture, his appearance ageless and simple. Red whiskers, sharp and thick, covered a long, hanging jaw whose bones seemed to be loose and out of their sockets.

Roe built a fire in the potbelly. Soon the poacher was warming his callused hands against the evening chill. "Don't worry, Mr. Watchman. I won't run amok on you. We're a special breed of stiff, not like the rest. We're the peaceable kind and we have a strong appetite for imp meat. What's more, I've got a proposition for you."

"Tell me what it is. I'm prepared to listen."

"If my stink bothers you, please say so."

"It isn't so bad yet."

"If it gets where you can't stand it, I've got some scented oil in my pouch. You can rub me down with it."

"All right. Now, a proposition you said?"

The poacher's mouth opened at intervals and his black tongue darted and quivered. "Yes, the proposition. It's quite a good one for you. Do you have any tea? I'm parched and drowsy."

After a cup of urpflanz tea and four starch bars, the stinker fell asleep on the floor near the fire.

"I suppose we'll talk in the morning," Roe said to himself, and retired to his pallet on the other side of the stove.

Some time during the night, a light awakened him. The poacher held a burning match at the face of an old wind-up clock ticking on the mantel. "What's that?" he asked. "Is it marking time?"

"Yes. It's called a clock."

"A clock?"

"The little hand tells the hour, the big hand tells the minutes."

"That makes no sense. An hour is big, a minute is little."

"What is your proposition? You say you have a letter from the Reverend? May I see it?"

The poacher produced a sheet of paper. "There it is. It gives me harvesting rights, signed by the Reverend himself. It's all for charity, you know. We feed a lot of city stinkers with the meat. I expect you'll abide by the document."

Roe lit a candle. "It looks official."

"That's the proposition. That you be shifted back to Bum Bay and I and my fellow workers will take over this tower. We need a place to rest and regroup after the harvest. This is an up-shift for you. You'll be in training at the Office of Parasite Control. Very cushy position. A load of responsibility."

"I can say without hesitation, I accept the proposal."

"Good. I'll be on my way."

"Will you join me for a little something to eat?"

"You got any imp?"

"Sorry, no."

"Urpmilk?"

Roe shook his head.

"All right, then. I'll be going now. Hope you like your new position."

"Have a safe trip."

The poacher made his way to the stairs and climbed down. Roe went out to the gallery to see him off. After squatting to defecate, the poacher climbed into his pedal car and waved. "The best of luck in your new position." The car rolled off down the road that went north, eventually, to Indian Apple.

Roe oiled his saw and packed his duffel that evening, pulled on his walking boots and took the same road on foot. After trekking two days and a night, resting, eating and bathing once at a roadside Templex, he arrived at the PC office just as they were opening their doors. His case officer, a square-faced American female with a bald head, interrogated him briefly.

"Any recent mouth-to-mouth contact with stinkers?"

"No."

"Anyone in your family or circle of friends infested with parasites?"

"My grandmother. She's at Permanganate Island. A mild case. She'll be getting early release."

"What is in that bag over your shoulder?"

"My saw."

"You're a carpenter. That's very handy around here."

"I play the saw with a bow. I don't know one nail or plank from another."

The officer stood up and took a set of keys from a hook behind her. "How very unusual. I'd like to hear that sometime, but right now I better show you the ropes."

Roe and the officer pedaled a van out of the PC garage and rolled across town to Grand Street, a posh neighborhood. The officer said, "I'll show you the ropes," and stopped before a nicely appointed home with a red tile roof and a granite chimney. "Now here's a typical situation," she said. "That's the Peterbilt mansion. These are stinkers with money and parasites. It's a situation crying out for some control."

A servant led them into the rear of the house and through the kitchen, where a maid was rinsing dishes. Mrs. Peterbilt, a third-stage stinker, entered in a white silk chemise, carrying an envelope. There was a pendulous growth on her throat, filled with parasites. One could see their movements through the flesh.

"You take the envelope from her," the officer said, "without making physical contact, and count what's in it."

Roe counted the bucks. "One hundred."

"That isn't half enough, Mrs. Peterbilt," the officer said, with extreme annoyance.

Mrs. Peterbilt begged for more time. "Please. You know my husband has been shifted. I'll be destitute if this keeps up. A hundred here, a hundred there."

"In a case like this," the officer explained to Roe, "when they fail to pay up, do something that hurts them. They don't feel much pain, so you have to be brutal. Hit her in the head with something, or kick her over and over again as hard as you can." The officer demonstrated her skill by taking two or three steps back, then charging forward with a kick to Mrs. Peterbilt's leg that cracked her brittle shin bone and dropped her to the floor.

"See, their bones are brittle. A hard kick to the shins will topple them like a stool with a broken leg."

"This is my work?"

"Yes, to put the squeeze on wealthy stinkers, to slowly drain them dry of financial resources. In return they get protection."

"From what?"

"Further harm, I suppose. I've never really wondered or asked. That's why I haven't been shifted in ages. They like me at the office."

"Does that hurt?" Roe asked Mrs. Peterbilt.

"Not much," she said, "but now I can't walk without help. How will I pick the bagworms off my cedar bush?"

"Where do the bucks go after I collect them?" Roe asked the officer.

"First they go from you to me, then I pass it on. I suppose sooner or later it ends up in the private account of Reverend Hooker. He deserves it above all and to the exclusion of every other."

"He's known for his witty sayings," Roe said.

"So he is. Now, go over and hurt that old sack of bones. You need practice. Make her tell you where the bucks are."

Mrs. Peterbilt still lay sprawled on the floor.

The maid and the servant had been watching these doings with interest, smiling, their arms folded. "Hurt her good," the servant said. "I like to see it." He held out a pair of poultry shears. "Cut something off her."

Roe took the shears, knelt beside the old stinker, placed her little finger between the blades and cut it nearly off by squeezing the handles as hard as he could. "My apologies, Mrs. Peterbilt, but I was shifted into this. Just doing what I'm told. Where do you keep your bucks?"

"I won't tell."

The officer nodded toward Roe. "Take it all the way off."

The first squeeze of the handle had not been enough to cut completely through the bone, so Roe placed the shears on the floor and stepped on the handle. This severed the finger completely. Mrs. Peterbilt groaned, then placed the slightly-bleeding stump into her mouth.

The officer rifled through kitchen cabinets, looked inside all the crockery. "Where've you hidden it?"

Mrs. Peterbilt had no response.

"Okay, Roe. Do something else to her. Show me what you're made of."

The maid held out an iron skillet. "Smash her head with this."

The servant stepped forward with a lit candle. "No, burn her face. She doesn't like that at all. She'll tell you where the bucks are."

Roe took the suggestion and held the flame just beneath her nose. Mrs. Peterbilt could only endure this a few

103

moments before giving up, turning from the flame, and crying, "It's under the begonia pot in the greenhouse."

"That's good, Roe," the officer said. "I think you'll be out on your own starting tomorrow. We'll get the bucks and go to lunch. The Impeteria's got stew on special, all you can eat."

After locating the begonia and collecting the bucks, the officer pried open Mrs. Peterbilt's mouth with a dinner knife. "You got any gold in there?" Finding none, she tossed the knife into the sink. "It's pretty common with these stinks," she told Roe. "Most of them have got some gold in their mouth. Always be sure to check. If they don't pay, you're authorized to pull teeth."

On the pedal to the café, Roe wondered whether this move to the Control office had been an up- or down-shift. "So, once more," he said to the officer, "what I'll be doing is taking money from wealthy stinkers and giving it to the Reverend?"

"Correct."

"And inflicting pain if they hedge."

"As much as necessary."

"I understand."

"When we get back to the office, I'll give you a voucher for three nights at the Gons Hotel. After that you'll have to find quarters of your own. Your pay will be fifty a week, on duty sunup to sunset every day. The Office will issue you a pedal car. Come see me in the morning and I'll give you your list for the day."

"A list of what, of wealthy stinkers?"

"Correct, and their addresses. Look in the trunk of the car you get. There're some tools of the trade in there, in a kit. Take it into the properties with you. It's got picks, blades, candles, a mallet, tooth pliers, fish hooks, brace and bit, sulfuric acid—be careful with that—and a ball peen hammer. You'll need to be issued some boots, too, with steel toes. Maybe you'll even want to use that saw of yours to take off a foot or a hand or something."

The Impeteria was crowded for the lunch hour. Dozens of pedal cars and Q-peds were parked side by side in the rear lot. In the hazy, still air, a plume of gray smoke rose undisturbed from a stack behind the clapboard building, and smelled faintly of cooked meat. Stinkers unloaded fresh-killed imps by the basketful from a pedal van parked at the rear. Beneath a sign saying "No Stinkers," a line had formed at the front door.

At seeing the sign, Roe felt a small degree of sympathy. "Things have gotten bad for the stinkers, haven't they?"

The officer placed a wog of willy in her mouth and swallowed it. "Worthless hunks of putrid flesh. You want some willy before we eat?" She pressed another wog of the red, clay-like material into Roe's palm. "It'll turn on your apostat."

Roe rolled the willy between his hands until it looked like a small sausage, then bit off portions and chewed them until the binder dissolved and released prickly little granules that irritated his throat as they went down. The irritation lasted only moments, replaced by an empty feeling in his stomach. "That stew sounds good," he said. "I hope they don't run out before we get a table."

"No tables," the officer said. "It's a stand-up place."

Roe stood tip-toe and looked into the café's window. He saw diners standing shoulder to shoulder and elbow to elbow. There were frequent spills of stew, spoons were dropped, and a noisy confusion of arms and hands was something of an impediment in the attempt to get the stew from bowl to mouth. Servings were being delivered from the kitchen to patrons by passing bowls from one set of uplifted hands to another. "That's mine!" someone shouted. "Over here!" another did, and the bowls changed direction.

"I'm a little claustrophobic," Roe said.

"Wait till the willy kicks all the way in. You'll be a people-person right away."

The line shortened slowly over a period of three or four hours as customers who were finished eating came out of a side door, the backs of their rags spattered with gravy, strings of meat clinging to their caps.

When the last person waiting in front of Roe had been pulled into the dining room and swallowed by the crowd, a cook came around from the kitchen door and addressed the still-waiting dozens in line. "Sorry, folks. We're all out. The stew is gone, the pots are washed, and we're closing up till breakfast tomorrow."

"This happens a lot," the officer said. "I don't know why I keep coming."

Roe said. "Let's go somewhere else. It's almost supper time."

"This is the only place still open." The officer dug her clog into the dirt and took her first step toward the van. "The last Chaos killed off most of the restaurants. The food got contaminated. Don't you read the papers?"

"I don't. I'm print blind. It runs in the family. Words on the page are a blur. My grandmother always read to me, but never the newspaper."

The officer lifted her shoulders one at a time, rotated her arms in their sockets and let out a long, weary breath. "All right, let's go back to the office and call it a day." The officer gave Roe another plug of willy. "Here, this much will turn off your apostat. You'll sleep. Go to your room at the Gons and come to work in the morning."

Roe rubbed the wog between his palms. "That suits me."

His room at the Gons was at street level, a little moldy and damp, but with a bunk bed high off the water-logged floor and accessible by a three-rung wooden ladder. To pass the evening hours, he sat in the top bunk and played the saw until his hand went numb, when he dropped his bow and fell back into a deep, willy-deep sleep.

When Roe reported to the Control Office in the morning, a different officer greeted him at the pedal car shed. "Good morning, Mr. Balls. The officer who showed you the ropes yesterday is no longer here. They shifted her to Permanganate last night. She's infested."

"I was to be given a list."

The new officer searched through a drawer that made a shrill sound when it was pulled out. "Here's a list of loaded stinkers. Is that it?"

"Yes."

"There's your car, over there, the black one. It pulls to the left. Be careful."

Roe put the car in neutral and pedaled in place to wind the spring and warm the sprockets while he looked over the list. There were three names and three posh addresses. The first, on Cherry Avenue, was Arlen Chips, a fourth-stage stinker who had made his fortune selling antique coffin silk to Reverend Hooker's parachute works.

Roe went to the front door with his bag of tools. From within the home, he heard a shrill, wavering sound, which he identified as a saw being poorly played. He rang the bell. When he did, the saw playing ceased and a maid answered the door.

"Good morning," Roe said matter-of-factly, a tone he had been instructed to use at this stage of the collection process. "I'll need to see Mr. Chips. I'm from the Parasite Control office."

The maid turned toward the dim, curtained interior. "Mr. Chips? There's a man from PC to see you."

A tall figure at the far end of a long hallway waved an envelope. "Come on in, son. I'm ready. I've got what you want. It's all right here in this envelope."

Roe looked at his list. "It says two hundred bucks."

"No, no." As the man came closer to the door, Roe could see that he was wearing a cloth bag over his head, which he lifted slightly when he spoke, showing several gold-capped teeth. "My regular payment is a hundred. It's been that way for years."

The maid nodded. "That's right. It's always been a hundred."

"I'm sorry, sir. It says two, as of today. We need another hundred."

"All right, Louise, let him in, then go out to the garden and get another hundred. I'm in no condition for a beating."

The maid showed Roe to a well-padded chair in the library. Mr. Chips came in with his saw and bow, walking sideways, then faced the wall and took the bag off his head. "Forgive me for coming in like a crab. I don't like showing my face to anyone. It'll be just a few minutes. Louise will dig up the bucks. Don't worry."

"That's good enough for me. I don't particularly like to hurt a stinker if I don't have to."

Mr. Chips said, "It's like skinning an imp. You'd rather not have to do it. But if you're hungry, that's another matter."

"It is," Roe agreed. "You play the saw. I heard you."

"What's that? My hearing's half gone and I'm facing away from you."

"I said you play the saw."

"I do try, but my arms are weak. It's just a screeching. Poor Louise patiently puts up with it."

Roe was about to let on that he played the saw himself when Louise returned from the garden with a metal box. Mr. Chips handed her a key. "Give him a hundred."

She opened the box and counted. "Five, ten, fifteen, twenty, thirty, forty . . . . Oh, dear. There's only fifty." She gave Roe that much, held the box upside down and shook it. "It's all there is."

Roe opened his bag of tools. "That's only half, Mr. Chips. I'll have to take out a couple of those teeth."

"Please," the maid said, "he only has a few left. He doesn't eat much, but without them, he'll have to be spoon fed."

"I'm only doing my job, Ma'am."

"Just a minute," Mr. Chips said. "I'll make this easier for all of us." He put the bag back in place, then banged his head on the wall and fell backward to the floor, his mouth conveniently open.

The first tooth came out of the gum with little effort on Roe's part and no blood. The second took a little moxie and more than a few hard tugs before it tore out of its dry socket. Mr. Chips showed no sign of pain or discomfort.

With the teeth in his pocket, Roe said goodbye to the maid and left the premises.

Eight.

After an evening together at the Bones Jangle a steam press operator and his stinker paramour returned to their hotel, The Gons, where he plunged a knife into his companion's body. She, in turn, quickly unsheathed the blade from her taut, sunken belly, and plunged her lover twice. Still, they laughed until other guests complained and Guards arrived. The bellboy turned the key in the lock and the two were dead before the door flew open. A note found in the stinker's purse indicated the bloody encounter was the result of a suicide pact, commonplace in the early days of any Chaos.

The Reverend has endorsed the theory that, because the earth has begun to wobble and list in its orbit, the lower half of the planet will eventually fall away, a cataclysmic event that would send the two halves striking for the stars separately, one to freeze, the other to burn. Meanwhile, the Reverend says he is going to re-calibrate the weight of the planet, now that we know roughly half of it will be gone: "To perform this measurement I'll take a pendulum to the Pole and note its vibration there. Then it must be taken to the Equator and the vibration there noted." After calculation, he admits, very little of scientific value would be known, "but something would have begun toward solving this mystery."

David Ohle

In Bum Bay, hopeless stinkers are hanging themselves from the belfry of the Templex, from lamp posts and from the eaves of dwellings. Bum Bayans can't leave their homes without seeing another one strung from a rafter tail, or swaying like a piece of meat from an awning, with imps licking at their feet. Living stinkers believe that when one of them is completely dead, the soul hovers near the body for forty or fifty days. So no one is willing to take them down until it is safe.

The Reverend has spoken out on the issue: "My people can't go out of their homes without seeing them hanging from the soffits like bats. On the pedal buses we see them swinging from the ceiling, their faces blue. They dangle from trees in Hooker Park, near the lagoon, swishing in the breeze, frightening children and drawing flies. This bad business hovers over us like a rain cloud. I'll find a way to stop them. That I can promise."

One of the most remarkable experiments in the indefinite prolongation of life in tissues by artificial methods, it became known today, is the specimen of a donor stinker's heart extracted at the Permanganate facility eight years ago. It has not only retained the spark of life, but has grown to many times its original size. The organism is still functioning and, disbarring accidents, will continue to grow indefinitely. The organism has been nourished regularly while cultured in an antiseptic solution.

You can survive a Chaos, says Wallace Hooker, who remains in guarded condition after a venomous snake bite, if you order one of his patented Hyberhomes. Pre-made of driftwood and pig iron, walls six inches thick, the structure measures ten by ten with a maximum occupancy of six and can be lowered into a backyard excavation. Along with the *Hyberhome, buyers receive a copy of Hooker's* Survival Tips for Chaotic Times, *a how-to manual for living in a stuffy Hyberhome for indefinite periods while Chaos rages above.*

An excerpt from Survival Tips: *"The Chaos has finally come. Now, what? Without one of my Hyberhomes, survival is a matter of luck. With one, it is almost guaranteed, provided you and your family can weather the stillness and boredom. That's what this manual is all about. First, as soon as the Chaos reaches your area, adults should escort the young children into the Hyberhome and explain to them that there will be a very bad period of depression for three or four days after the door is closed and sealed. After the shock has worn off and the dreadful monotony of life underground sets in, activity is one of the best remedies. Each person should have regular tasks to perform. In the off-duty periods, there should be reading, games, willy-taking, anything to keep from dwelling over-much on one's self. After the depression passes, there will be a notable lift in spirits. Talk will turn to planning what to do when the all-clear signal is broadcast: rebuilding homes, putting out fires, disposing of corpses, and planting a garden. When this happens, you are over the hump."*

Reports from Pisstown detail a series of hair thefts. Young females, grown females, long-haired males are all potential victims. The thief pulls them down to the sidewalk and applies a sanitary napkin soaked with chloroform to their faces. This behavior has been described many times by his shaven subjects. Some say he mumbles in a barely articulate manner when he works his magic with razor and scissors. He has not injured anyone beyond minor abrasions and superficial cuts, although an overdose of chloroform did completely kill a young male stinker, third-stage. Some say he mumbles his name, which sounds

111

like Ozalo, perhaps Oxward or Oswald. Guards are fearful of what they might find when the hair thief is finally caught and his quarters entered for searching.

What then is a final-stage stinker's life like? It has been described by scientists as showing a poverty of sensation and a low body temperature. In their nostrils is the persistent odor of urpmilk. The membrane which lines their mouth is extremely tough and is covered with thick scales. They like to touch fur and drink their own urine. Because they have been known to go without food for as long as eighteen years, we can assume that their sense of time passing is also very different from our own.

Less than a week after Jacob Balls's fatal fall, which occurred just a day before his sixtieth birthday, Mildred appeared at the Pisstown Templex to file a lawsuit. There was every reason to believe his death was not an accident.

"Take a number, please," the receptionist said without lifting her gaze. "What grievance brings you to this office?"

"I plan to sue the RPC."

"The Reverend's Parachute Company?"

"Yes."

"Your claim against them?"

"My husband's death. The parachute was demonstrably flawed. It failed to open."

"You'll see the first available counselor. Give me your hand, the back of it. You need a number."

Mildred held out her hand, palm down. The receptionist used a rubber stamp to ink the number seventy-three onto her liver-spotted flesh. "Seventy three? But I'm the only person here."

"Pay no attention to that. The numbers are not in order. We're very busy and we have no time to waste. We call the numbers randomly, too, so everyone has an equal chance."

"In other words, arriving early is rather pointless."

"No rhetorical gymnastics, please. I'd appreciate it if you'd speak to me plain and simple."

"The Reverend killed my husband. I want to press charges."

"Didn't you say it was a faulty parachute that killed your husband?"

"That was the proximate cause in a causal chain going directly to Reverend Hooker."

"That's enough of your smart talk. Please sit down. It may be a long wait." She handed Mildred a pad and pencil. "Use the time to write down the details of your case against the Reverend's company. In doing so, you should know beforehand that no one has ever prevailed in a legal tangle with Reverend Hooker. And you won't either."

Mildred sat down and pulled together her thoughts on the matter:

After Jacob took early retirement three years ago, he began to parachute for the thrill and pleasure of it. On the 4th of July last he attempted to parachute into Hooker Park with fatal consequences.

That day the butler pedaled the children and me to the park for a picnic. Jacob was going to dive right into the picnic grounds and the butler was going to roast an imp and make an urpflanz salad.

At about noon we saw an orbigator overhead, as high as a thousand feet I would guess. It was leaving a little trail of steam, or smoke. Roe said, "Look, Mildred, the door is opening. He's ready to jump."

A moment later we saw him leap from the orbigator into the air. He was just a small spot in the glare of the sun. When he was about halfway down, we heard him scream. "It's not opening! It won't open!" We saw him frantically pulling on the cord. I was frozen, I couldn't move. The children's faces

113

were ashen. We heard Jacob's last desperate shout, "Sue the company!"

Then he struck the ground a few feet away. We heard every bone in him break. His lungs popped like balloons. It was a terrible shock and I intend to carry out his last wish, to take legal action against the Reverend, who owns the parachute company.

As Mildred sat composing, other would-be litigants entered the Templex legal office and were stamped with numbers. By the time she was finished, half the room's chairs were taken. After an hour's wait, the receptionist, who had been enjoying cat naps, called, "Number seventy-four? Where is seventy-four?"

An American standing in the rear came forward. "That's me." After a brief discussion with the receptionist, he sat next to Mildred. "It's cockeyed, the way things are done around here, isn't it? She's given me all this paperwork to fill out. I'm Frank. Pleased to meet you." He sat down and began to complete the paperwork.

"Mildred Balls. Likewise. What's *your* complaint?"

"I got side-shifted, did five years living in a broken-down movie house. Now I'm willy addicted and I drink enough Jake every day to drown an elephant. My digestive processes have stopped. At times I can hardly breathe. I'm going to sue the Reverend's shifting authority. And yours?"

"One of his parachutes killed my husband. The fall broke every bone in his body. The grandchildren were traumatized for life."

"That's fairly common lately, isn't it, those faulty parachutes. I'm sure it's intentional. They tell me the Reverend loves to get out there with his spyglass and watch them fall. It's a sport for him. Please, excuse me now while I do my paperwork. They say nobody ever wins these suits."

Five hours and twenty-two numbers later, long after the American had been in and out, seventy-three was called. "That's me," Mildred said. She'd sat so long her legs had fallen asleep and when she stood up, she toppled over and fell onto the worn wooden floor, driving several splinters into her face. She rolled onto her back and pumped her legs, as if pedaling, until sensation returned. The receptionist watched all this with mild interest, but made no effort to help. "I'll be fine," Mildred said, turning over and getting on her knees, then standing unsteadily.

"The attorney will see you now, Mrs. Balls. He apologizes in advance for being a little bilious today, so bear with his belching. Now, go down the hallway and it's the first door to the right. No, the left. Wait, no, it's the right. It's the last door on the right, as I said."

Mildred tried the knob on the first door to the right. It was locked. Through a frosted glass window she could see an empty desk with its drawers open and a wastebasket full of yellow, shredded, pre-edible paper.

She tried the last door on the left. It was open and she entered a dark room that was extremely cold. A bright light came on when the heavy door closed, revealing a pale, sickly-looking stinker in a business suit, sitting on a rickety bench with a yellow pad in his lap and a fountain pen in his hand. Beside the bench was a wastebasket, also full to the spilling-over point with balled-up sheets of yellow paper.

"You're number seventy-three and you want to sue the Reverend?"

"Yes."

"Sit down then." There was no place other than next to the attorney on the bench.

"It's very cool in here, isn't it?" she said.

The attorney burped acidly. "It keeps the stink down, the cool does. Used to be too warm in here. One of the boilers exploded last year. The heat doesn't come this far any more. I'm well adapted to it but I can understand how you might find it uncomfortable. If it becomes too unpleasant to continue, we can re-schedule at another time. I have some open dates in the latter part of next year."

"I'll continue."

"Fine, let me see your complaint. And let me know if my smell offends you. I have some scented oil handy if it does."

Mildred gave him her written account and he read it over quickly. "You must understand, Mildred, the Reverend will argue that your husband never tried to open the main chute. He will argue that it was a suicide. You won't get far in the higher courts with a claim of faulty parachute, not against the Reverend's legal muscle. I suggest you drop this claim immediately." He balled up her account and threw it into the wastebasket among all the others.

"I'm not prepared to do that. I'm determined to press this claim."

"We can't help you at all. I'm sorry. This office is not sanctioned to handle cases like this. You can plainly see how understaffed we are."

"Then what is a person to do?"

"I can tell you only this, that when the neighborhood judiciaries were set up, the intent was not to bring cases forward but to bottle them up at street level. All crime is local. And so is punishment."

"I suppose I have no more business here, then," Mildred sighed, getting up from the bench. "I'll be going now, to look for other channels to petition for legal action."

"All the luck in the world is what you'll need. I hope you understand the mission of the neighborhood judiciaries a little better than you did before."

"I do, I do."

Nine.

Roy "Gluefoot" Bishop, eighteen years old, is the young-
est Guard to die in the Reverend's service. He was run
over by a Pisstown pedal bus at Second and Central on
Thursday, while in pursuit of an imp which had escaped
from a woman who was carrying it in a cage and lodged
itself in the eaves of a nearby precinct building. Bishop,
known for his remarkable climbing abilities, helped by a
running start, walked fifty feet up the side of a brick wall,
took the imp by its feet, walked down again, and tumbled
into the wheels and gears of the passing bus. The imp
survived but was never captured.

Not many times has Wallace Hooker been seen in pub-
lic of late. Those who have been so lucky describe him
as smaller in stature than they had imagined, with a
face that is pale, drawn, and dotted with liver spots
and weeping sores. He has been seen sleeping in gutters,
snoring like a buzz saw and attracting flies. He has been
spotted in alleyways eating garbage. And that's not all, the
Reverend said yesterday. "He has taken his Q-ped all the
way to Indian Apple, frequented brothels and engaged in
other revelries too sordid to repeat."

During an unscheduled appearance by Reverend Hooker in
Witchy Toe, an anti-Hookerite rushed out of the audience

and slapped him repeatedly across the cheeks and then escaped through a back exit in the midst of the confusion. No one was surprised. When the Reverend makes a public appearance these days, it's like a falling leaf breaking the surface of a pond. It awakens creatures long asleep at the bottom.

Recovered from the slapping, the Reverend gave this statement to reporters: "The town is frolicsome tonight. It's just a bagatelle. I remain joyful and confident."

The miscreant who did the slapping was apprehended and taken into custody and will be dispatched to the Templex for a parasite check, and then to Permanganate for a long, unhurried stay.

A charcoal burner who, about a year ago, was shifted to Indian Apple, attempted to kill his family with a hand-sickle. A third-stage stinker, he returned to his cabin at about ten a.m. and said to all members of his family but his son, who was out shoveling coal, "I have just taught myself to use this tricky sickle and now I want all of you to stand up." In order to humor him, they rose. He tied their hands with a piece of cord, which he knotted on the rafters. Holding the sickle, he commenced cutting his family, inflicting some dreadful wounds.

As he completed his work, his son returned, covered in coal dust, and was alarmed by what he saw. Chasing his father from the cabin, the son then went back to help his severely injured loved ones.

A posse was formed, but as yet the charcoal burner remains at large.

An early traveler on the National Canal described Permanganate thus: "There is a small island in the Canal a hundred miles downstream from Pisstown on which no vegetation or animation can exist. Bones that have drifted to the island invariably turn to ashes within eight to ten days. One imp has ossified merely by lapping the water in a stagnant ditch. Box turtles anchoring at the island to sunbathe on its logs have suddenly gelled and dripped away like candle wax. Caustic permanganate in the soil is blamed both for its odd violet color and its toxicity."

Moldenke is in Indian Apple, appearing nightly at the Imperial. His earthly father's head is pickled in a jar onstage beside him. In some way Moldenke is not only able to make its lips move, but to reproduce his father's voice with perfect fidelity. Moldenke tells the audience he is "in his father's head" when he spins his long yarns of the world beyond. After every tale the head solicits contributions in a bubbling voice and the mouth spits a coin into the fluid to encourage tithing. "Please give generously," it says. "Only in that way will I be kept alive."

Not long after Ophelia was shifted, other shiftees began to arrive at the Balls mansion. With Templex records listing it as abandoned property, it was only a matter of a few days before all the rooms were spoken for, even the butler's quarters, and noisy children were sliding down the banisters and screaming with excitement.

Red moved into the potting shed with Peters and fashioned a bed out of peat, straw and sheets stolen from the clothesline. "I don't know who owns this bedding," he told Peters, who didn't mind sleeping on the bare ground, "but as sure as Hooker is the American Divine, they owe it to me. After all, I cook for fifty or sixty every night and empty their chamber pots every morning. Two sheets is no great loss, and I richly deserve them."

The pantry in the main house kitchen was soon empty, all the wild-picked urpflanz gone, and the basement larder devoid of anything but rat droppings. Red was at a loss as to how he would continue to feed his unwanted but needy guests. "Too bad Mrs. Balls is gone to Permanganate. She would have thought of a way to cope with this. We've already trapped all the imps on the property."

Peters said, "I'll go into town and get a breeding pair. We'll raise them in cages. "

"What will we feed them?" Red asked.

"We'll just have to find stinkers that want to be put down. That's all they eat nowadays is dead stinkers. They lost their taste for grass somehow."

"Putting down a stinker is dirty business," Red said. "I won't do it."

"Heck, all you have to do is tie them up. I'll put them down."

"All right then."

Peters walked to the far edge of Pisstown, taking circuitous routes to avoid the still-smoldering fires of the Chaos. The city abattoir always had a pen reserved for sickly imps that were sold cheaply. Peters picked out the two best-looking ones and told the clerk he wanted a pair of breeders. "We've got shiftees up to the neck out at the Balls place. They've got to have some meat once in a while."

"You don't want those two. They're old, half-spent. I've got a much better deal for you. This is a one time offer, for your ears only."

"I'm listening."

"How many bucks you got?"

"I got ten."

"Come over and look at these little experimental imps I've got here. It's a mating pair. The Reverend's raising them on a commercial basis. Not only will the female bear six young a year, they'll re-meat. You go in there, in their pen, and you say, 'Dinnertime,' they'll come right on over and show you their butt end. You cut off whatever you want. There's a little bleeding involved, but even that can be used in making bloodwursts. And by the next morning the same little imp can give you enough fresh bacon to feed twenty or thirty."

When Peters leaned over the pen to look the imps over, they were lying still, side by side, asleep. He saw raw places on their hindquarters in the process of re-meating. "What's their weight?"

"Twenty each right now. They'll top at a hundred or so when they grow up. The Reverend guarantees them for twelve years. If one fails to re-meat, I'll refund your money or give you another pair."

"How much you want?"

"Ten for two. This is an introductory offer. Like I said, they're not really on the market yet. That's why they're cheap."

"What will we feed them?"

"That's the beauty of this new kind of imp. You don't feed them anything. They feed on one another. And they'll eat their own feces, too."

The clerk stunned the two imps with a mallet and put them into sacks, which Peters carried across his shoulders at the ends of a wooden yoke.

Before starting the long walk back to the mansion, he stopped to drink a Jake or two at the Zig Zag Lounge, just down the road. As soon as he entered, having left his imps in the alley, he saw Roe sitting in a bright cone of smoky afternoon light that poured through a jagged hole in the roof. His once-blonde hair was a dark, tangled mess, yet his face had been scrubbed raw with pumice-soap and he'd doused himself with an odor retardant.

"Hello there, young Roe. Long time no see," Peters said.

"Who are you?"

"Peters, the yard man. Don't you remember me?"

"Oh, yes, Peters."

Roe ordered a pitcher of Jake and an extra glass. "I'm dying of thirst. I've already had three Jakes and I haven't quenched it yet."

"You look a bit rough, Roe."

"I might have the parasite. I'm not sure. I'm weak. And I've been shifted again. This time to Witchy Toe. I'll be working in a willy plant. Back breaking, probably. I thought I'd rest up at the house for a few days."

Peters drank the last of the pitcher, rinsed his mouth with Jake, then spit it on the floor. "There's no room there, Roe boy. We're up to our necks in shiftees. Not a bed left. Things up there are as sorry as things can get. The septic tanks overflowed a while back and leeched into the well. The only thing that comes out of the faucets is a sticky drizzle of yellow algae. So we sure could use some rain. The pond is so dry the fish have died. Your poor grandmother, she's going to faint away when she sees what happened while she was gone."

"Thank you for the information, sad as it is. I'll get a room at the Orienta."

"I better get going," Peters said. "I've got a pair of little imps to carry back."

"So long, Peters. Nice to see you again."

"Ditto, old friend." Peters crumpled a few bucks onto the bar and left through a side door, letting in the sound of imps squealing, chirping and barking.

Roe asked the barkeep if there was a public privy in the area.

"Down the street a couple of blocks, past Hobson's stable and through the Heritage Area. It's kitty-corner from the Impeteria."

There was a heavy fog in the air when Roe stepped outside. He could see the dull glow of a street lamp in the distance and headed that way, tripping on curbs, stepping on slugs, but eventually finding the privy. Lighting a candle and sitting on one of the two holes, he counted his bucks. There would be expenses in getting to Witchy Toe.

When the counting was over, he had sixty-two bucks, barely enough even if he pinched his pennies every step of the way. He rolled the bucks into a manageable wog and in the process of trying to stuff it back into his pocket, let it fall into the other hole. He heard a single plop as it landed on top of the waste. He quickly wiped himself with one of the urpflanz leaves provided by the city and lowered his candle into the hole. There it was, the roll of bucks, stuck in the waste.

Those of a different mind than Roe's perhaps would have abandoned the bucks or devised a safe and clean way to retrieve them. But Roe chose to extend one arm into the hole along with his head and a shoulder. That position left him short of the bucks by only a few inches. The candle's light shining through the other hole was enough illumination for him to judge the distance and gain confidence that he would be successful if he squeezed himself a little further in. When he tried to reach the bucks this time, he fell in head first. After righting himself, he remained there, standing with his arms folded through the long summer night in waste up to his navel.

After Guards pulled him out with a block and tackle the next morning, Roe had just enough time before his arrest on charges of "privy dipping" to splash himself with water from a stagnant puddle before being taken to the lockup and placed in a cell. When the wig's assistant came to take his deposition, she presented him the paper and pencil tied to the end of a thin pole. "Don't come any closer," she said. "You stink like the devil himself."

"They pushed me in here and left. I haven't had food or water for three days. My clothes are stiff with this dry waste. My candle is burning out. Please, help me. If I had a tub of water and some floating soap I could clean myself. I need water and food, badly."

"Yes, indeed. Just give us a deposition. Write down what happened, how you ended up in the muck, and I'll see if I can get the charges dropped. I don't see any criminal intent here. Your name is?"

"Balls. They call me Roe."

"Oh, one of the Balls heirs. That puts a different light on all this. The Balls family was negligent in helping finance the Reverend Hooker's consolidation of power, and that may close all the loopholes."

"Really. I didn't know that. I was often kept in the closet. That's why I'm so pale and pasty, even now. Mildred had a cruel streak. Grandfather was a lush, a spendthrift and a bore. I've had a bad life. I do love my sister, though. She made sure I had my colonics every day."

"I feel sorry for you. I'll still talk to the wig. I'll still see what I can do."

"That's decent. I'm grateful, but a little weak. I'm delirious."

"I'll get you some food and water. Hurry and write before your candle gutters."

Roe wrote:

It is not fair that I have been charged with the crime of privy dipping. How I came to be in that place was certainly a regrettable accident. There was no pleasure intended, nor was any enjoyed. The second time I tried reaching down to get my bucks, that's when I went in. I had my head, my right arm and shoulder down through the hole and I was holding on to the rim of the hole with my left hand. I needed that money to get to Square Island. I was going to pick the bucks up between my ring finger and my pinkie. I actually got my fingers on a corner of it and I was starting to lift it up, away from the waste, when I felt myself start to slip. I tried to pull my body back up, but I couldn't do it. The hand that was holding me up had gotten numb. The next thing I knew, I was in the hole. Head first. Straight to the bottom. The top of my head hit the hard mud and I fell over backwards. But I wasn't hurt too badly, except I'd scraped my hip on the way in. It's a good thing I didn't go unconscious. When I stood up I shook the waste off and wiped it away

from my eyes and I was glad there was a bottom to stop
me and that I was still alive, that I hadn't drowned in
the waste. I was completely covered. My whole body
had been under. The splash from my fall put out the
candle and I was in total darkness. I stood there a few
minutes trying to understand what had happened, and
think about how to get out. The stuff was about four
feet deep. I couldn't tell how big the pit was. But it
was all mud, sides and bottom. It was about the size
of a small jail cell, only underground and half full of
waste. I held up my arm and I could touch the edge
of the hole, but I couldn't get enough of a grip to pull
myself out. I tried to jump up and reach through the
hole and get a better grip, but it was impossible. I had
hit my collarbone hard on the edge of the hole going in
and I couldn't do any jumping. That's when I got sick
and vomited the first time. After that I walked around
to see if there might be something under the waste I
could stand on. The waste was thick at the bottom and
the top was liquid, the top foot or so. I kept my arms
folded all the time. That way they weren't dangling
down in the waste. I couldn't tell how fast time was
passing. I started screaming for help. "Help me, I'm
stuck!" It sounded loud in the pit, but I don't know
how it sounded outside. Then my throat got sore
and I had to stop yelling. I think I yelled for about
two hours, but no one came. Then I started pacing
around. I took a couple of steps in one direction,
then a couple of steps in another direction as if I
was in a cell. It must have been a hundred and ten in
that hole. I was sweating. It was a steam bath. I was
hot and I was nervous. I was in a state of shock. But
there wasn't anything more to do. I just stood there
with my arms folded, leaning against the side, waiting
for the sun to shine through that hole. My legs got
tired, but I was too frightened to get sleepy. If I had
fallen asleep I might have drowned. What's odd is, I

got sick a couple more times and the stink subsided. All I could smell was my vomit. Finally the waste on my face hardened enough that I could brush it off with my hand. Then I worried I might not get out of there at all. I was hallucinating. I thought I might deteriorate if I stayed in there too long. I thought that the waste might start rotting my skin. I worried about catching diseases. But the main thing I started worrying about was, what will Grandmother think when I get out? I was humiliated, extremely shamed. I was mortified. I thought about suicide. It might not be worth getting out if Grandmother was going to tease me and make fun of me. And I knew she would. I felt like ending my life right there. It wasn't worth coming out. I figured they wouldn't find my body, that it would just rot away in the muck. They would think I'd been kidnapped or something worse. Or if they did retrieve my body, it would be a black mark on the Balls family name. But I didn't kill myself. I waited, and I cried until the dawn finally came and I saw the first light through the hole, the hole that led up to life, real life, not life in the pit. There wouldn't have been much air coming in without that hole. I stood under it all night and breathed. With morning I thought someone might be walking by and I started screaming again, "Help me, I'm stuck." In a while two Guards strolled by and heard me. One of them came into the privy and said, "Where are you?" I said, "I'm down here! Look in the hole." I held my hand up so he could see it. It was still a little dark in the hole. He said, "Oh, I'll get a chain." In about an hour he came back with a chain and a few stinkers and they pulled me out.

The assistant appeared with a bucket of water, a chunk of floating soap, a starch bar, and bad news. "Well, Roe, I hate to tell you this, but the deposition won't do you any good. The charges will stick, the wig said. You'll appear before her right after you eat some starch and wash up. More bad news . . . this wig is a strict Hookerite. She doesn't listen to reason and she has no pity. I think your goose may be cooked. I'll be back to get you in ten minutes."

The words of the chief wig were intended to educate as well as rebuke and frighten. "Privy dipping is nothing to laugh at, Mr. Balls. You could be hanged for this. We could strip off your flesh and drop you in a tub of vinegar. Or we could let you off easy and send you to the Ice Palace for a public spanking."

"That would be my choice, the latter."

"These public spankings are conducted for a reason, and that reason is best exemplified by the words of Reverend Hooker, to wit, 'Humility is the mother, nurse, foundation and bond of all virtue.' You understand that?"

"Yes, Miss."

"But this is far too grievous for a spanking. I could send you to the prison at Permanganate Island. I could say, 'Off to the Purple Isle with you.' Do you want that?"

"Not at all, not at all."

"What did the Reverend's Book say about all this?"

"I don't know," Roe confessed.

"'We die that we die no more!'"

"Yes, I've heard that. I just didn't remember."

"As the chief wig in this area, I say you will move yourself and all your possessions, lock, stock and barrel, to the town of Witchy Toe. You'll be leaving tonight." The wig turned to an assistant. "Do we have a job for him there?"

"Yes, we do. He'll be working for the Reverend."

The job awaiting Roe was folding parachutes at the Reverend's Parachute Company. Some of them were intentionally folded so that they would tangle, it was explained in training, and the jumper would experience a fatal fall. Chutes with this intentional flaw were specially made for one of the thrill clubs in Pisstown, whose members, thirty or forty at a time, would jump from an orbigator. Most of them were victims of parasite infestation who wanted to be put down in an exciting way. Certain chutes failed, usually a third of them, others didn't.

"It's Russian roulette with a twist," the trainer explained, "The thing is, we don't want the chutes getting mixed up. Because of their intended use, we won't be putting labels on them. Once they reach the end of the line, no one can tell which is which. The ones who survive can then look forward to the thrill of the next jump."

During this shift, Roe lived in a frigid, tin-roofed lean-to behind Zeus Bologna Company and worked long hours at the parachute factory. His supervisor, Mr. Enso, a proud and proper Hookerite, often tried to convert him. "All right, Balls. You're a good worker. I'll grant you that. But you're the only one here who hasn't joined up. Why don't you go on down to the Templex and put your Jerry Hancock on the dotted line?"

"I would, Mr. Enso, but my grandmother would never approve."

"Your *grand*mother?"

"It would kill her to know I'd become a Hookerite. Sorry, I can't do it."

"Go back to work, you uncooperative shit, you!"

"Yes, sir."

On Mondays, the only day the P.P.C. was closed, Roe would sit in Witchy Toe's Hooker Park and feed starch bar pieces to banty imps. Several of them would perch on the back of his bench and stroke his hair as he fed them. Aside from this small diversion, Roe's life had become a dreary, humdrum drag, a damper on his already guttering spirit. Then the Chaos came. It was small-scale, but violent and disruptive. Factories were shut down, including the P.P.C. People wishing to be reasonably safe remained behind locked doors, venturing out only to get whatever food and water was available. The starch bar factory fast became a charnel house.

In great numbers the severely wounded and the sick-and-tired were taken there and left to die. There were so many, a five-acre meadow east of town was commandeered for use as a burial pit.

When winter came, this Chaos, like others, lost its momentum for a time. The carnival came to Witchy Toe for its winter engagement in the midst of the period of relative order, of the type that always foreshadowed a period of intensified Chaos. Shops were doing business, the streets were being cleaned, the corpses burned. Vendors offered Jake by the glass, starch bars, gel cans, matches, candles, bundles of urpflanz and limited supplies of willy.

Roe ventured out for the first time in months. He went into the post office and stood in line at the General Delivery window. "Anything for Balls?"

"We've been closed for a while, my friend. But that name, Balls. I remember that. There was something for you. It looked like shifting orders to me." After a half-hour's search through seven or eight mail sacks, the clerk found the orders. "Here they are. I was right, it's from the shifting office."

Roe opened the crisp, white envelope by sliding his thumb along the seal, cutting himself slightly. "I hope it's an up-shift for a change."

The order read:

SUBJECT: Order to Relocate
Dear Mr. Balls,

The Reverend requests that you report to the Balls summer estate on Square Island by Aug. 10. There you will serve under the head of mining operations. Additional instructions will be conveyed to you upon your arrival.

Your faithful servant,
Reverend Herman Hooker

129

Roe took the orders with him into the street and bought a glass of Jake from a vendor. "Looks like I'm going to the old Island place," he said. "It's more or less home. Hallelujah. Now and then the shiftings make sense."

The vendor filled a glass with water and stirred in Jake powder. "All we got is water. No urpmilk. Big Chaos. But the ice house opened up yesterday, so the water's cold."

Roe drank the first glass down and asked for another. "I'll leave right away. I'll take the pedal tram tonight. But may I ask you something?"

The vendor served the second glass. "Certainly, ask away."

"It says I'm to work in a mining operation. I wonder what they're mining."

"Probably teeth. They're finding veins of them all over the place. Hooker needs gold for all those altar pieces, the gold thread in the vestments, all that."

"Teeth mining? I hadn't heard of it."

"You will. You will."

Ten.

An urpflanz farmer who lives one mile north of Pisstown informed this correspondent that a demented imp spent the day with him on his farm. He saw it several times, chasing down his diminutive rat hound. He claims the animal is of prodigious size and of a gregarious nature, even playful. "It didn't want to eat my little hound. It wanted to play with him." The imp had a brass bell tied around its neck with a cord, presumably to warn of its approach. After a few minutes, the farmer says, the little hound sensed the imp's intentions were benign and joined in play, delightedly chasing, then being chased.

The Reverend, campaigning near the camp at Witchy Toe, has been hypnotized by steel. A barber started to shave him, but the moment the blade touched the Reverend's throat, his muscles relaxed. He was thought dead. After thirty minutes had gone by, a client of the shop gave him a snapping thump with a middle finger on the bridge of his nose and this revived him. The Reverend later said, "I have often fallen into a hypnotic state in the barber's chair. The little snip-snip of the scissors, the gentle touch of the comb, the pleasant shock of warm shaving soap, the sweet smell of the tonics and talcums. It all comes together and puts me in a state of reverie. So, go out and vote on voting day with confidence. Have no fear about your Reverend's state of health."

A crazed stinker female has taken up residence under the Bum Bay swing bridge. She is a slinky woman who comes at children from a low ditch under the bridge with mud caked to her hair. Because her hand is usually palsied, she straps a plaster model of a hand to her wrist to alarm her natural enemies: boys with switches, girls with sticks, old men with rods. Sometimes she picks young men up from the spot where they stand and carries them off. She kills them after kissing them, then rides to the nearest town and dumps the bodies in front of the Guard station or the Templex.

A ten-inch parasite has been taken from the foot of Wallace Hooker. There had been swelling and pain and he thought it was rheumatism, but his entire constitution became affected. He grew adipose, his disposition declined to such an extent that he was taken by Q-ped to a sanitarium. There the flesh burst and the parasite was revealed. Hooker claimed the parasite's presence had caused his face and hands to draw in such a way as to make them useless. He says that he had spent a great deal of time working in the tooth mine outside Pisstown and that the parasite probably entered through a lesion on his heel then. He has heard of instances when the parasites passed from one part of the body of the victim to another, and he attributes the fever and chills he suffered to this migratory action. After removal, the gigantic parasite was put in a pail of brine and kept for observation.

Two imp hunters tramping through the woods near Witchy Toe nearly stepped into a sinkhole more than four hundred feet wide and two hundred feet deep, another collapse of substrata, one of many in the area. When the hunters were gagged by a rouge-colored, sulfurous vapor rising from the hole, they fled, seeking help. From a safe distance, Witchy Toe residents watched the goings on. As soon as the vapors ceased to rise, an assortment of artifacts was collected from the slurry at the bottom, including the cloth-bound remains of a male child stuffed into a wooden nail keg and more than two tons of tooth gold.

The death traveler, Moldenke, startled a seeress in Bum Bay when he knocked at her door and asked, "Is that your cockatiel speaking to me from the camphorberry tree?" The seeress immediately saw the bird, which rasped, "All aboard!" It was not her bird, she told him, and dispatched him with a sweep of her broom. Later, after she had taken her afternoon nap, she found Moldenke asleep on her porch glider. When she awakened him, he began to sing as he backpedaled from the premises in a peaceful manner. "I was once a famous man," he shouted, then turned to walk facing forward. "My name was Sinatra then and my crooning was known around the world. Now I'm looking for work, any work."

Before the day was out, an elderly stinker appeared in the seeress's yard. She looked out the window and saw him, a tall one, feeding crackers to the cockatiel. She opened the window and gave him a warning. "You get out of my yard or I'll take a skillet to your head."

The lanky stinker said, "My apologies, lady, but I'm only looking for my friend, Moldenke. He might have said his name was Sinatra. Have you seen him? I know he's in these parts somewhere. The Chaos is over. We're looking for work. He was famous, you know."

"I just sent him down the road," she replied, "And I'll do the same to you." She stepped onto the porch and hefted her broom. "Go! Get!"

The stinker complied with her wishes, but said in going, "I once ruled the world from my hotel room, you know. I flew aircraft. One had eight engines and was made of wood."

The cockatiel then repeated its refrain, "All aboard!" and the second stinker began hoofing long-legged along the road.

Mildred Balls was released from the Permanganate Island Facility on Coward's Day and was the last in line to get a ticket for the return trip. The *Noctule* was crowded with rough riders on the way to Pisstown for the celebration. She was lucky to find a seat in the commissary, which bustled with hungry, Jake-fueled rough riders eating stewed imp brains and bragging.

"Come tomorrow I'm gonna get me one of those yellow bellies and I'm going to bite off his big red nose and spit it back at him."

"Me, I'll kick some asses with these heavy-soled boots."

"You boys are awfully easy on them cowards. Here's what I'm going to do. I'm going to take my pocket knife and stick it in one of their ears and twist it in as far as it'll go."

Having no interest in their brutal concerns, Mildred tried to avoid eye contact with them, but by the time she had taken only a few bites of the poorly prepared stew, they had begun to pry.

"What were you in for, lady?"

"Parasites."

"That's bad. Prison's better."

"It was a light infestation. A spider bite proved to be the cure. I'm free of them."

"You been there long?"

"Years. I'm looking forward to seeing my grandchildren again if I can find them. They've been shifted all over creation."

"We're all Hookerites. You a Hookerite?"

"No. I never saw the appeal."

"You planning to hurt a coward tomorrow?"

"No."

"You like that stew?"

"Compared to Permanganate Island, it's very elegant. Compared to the way I used to make it, it's fit for the slop jar."

The stew in Mildred's bowl spilled when the *Noctule* suddenly leaned to one side, then the other, as its balsa screws began to spin in their cowlings. The big orbigator lifted unevenly from the field and passengers held onto whatever could be grasped. When it settled into a smooth ascent, a team of stinkers came from the kitchen to clean up the spills.

When Mildred bid the rough-riders goodnight, they raised their glasses of Jake to her. "Hip, hip, hooray, old girl. You're a pip."

"Thank you. I'm very sleepy. I'm turning in."

"Okay then. We'll kick a coward for you tomorrow."

Mildred settled into a chair on the open-air outer deck and, despite the stormy roar of the ship's screws, slept until the jolt of the *Noctule's* landing woke her up and one of the crew told her, "You better get off the ship in a hurry, lady. We don't stay here long." Mildred took up her bag and descended the gantry stairs as quickly as she could, sometimes being swept downward by the crowd, her feet dangling in air.

The nearest Templex to the landing field was a mile-long walk on rocky ground. Mildred's ankles were swollen twice their size when she got there, huffing and anxious, lilting with heat prostration. She knew there would be hours of paperwork ahead, then several more exhausting hours on the pedal bus. There had been a time, under conditions like these, when she would have been met by someone on her household staff with a fast, easy-to-pedal, four-seater Q-ped for the trip to the mansion. It was not a particularly busy day at the Templex, however, and Mildred was able to apply for a travel permit in relatively short order.

"Where to?" The clerk's face was partially obscured by a metal screen.

"The Balls estate, at the end of Outerditch Road."

"And your business there? Household service?"

"I'm Mildred Balls. It's my home."

"Oh, then I could probably expedite the paperwork for you, but my people tell me it's become a major shifting hub, the Balls place has. My brother knows the yard man up there. He told me all about it."

"I was afraid of that."

"He said Peters said you ought to be going to Square Island when they let you out. There's no room at the mansion."

"The Square Island house is boarded up. Every critter, bug and rodent on Earth is probably living there."

"The Reverend's shifting programs are in high gear, you know. Some places are being emptied, some are far too full. Another Chaos broke out in Pisstown last night. They say it's coming this way. Populations are pretty stirred up. Nerves are getting frazzled. You'll be fine on the Island. It's not expected to spread there."

"I weathered the last big Chaos on the Island. There were a few scuffles, some killings, fires, other minor disturbances, but there was a relative calm. Could it be the salty air and the gentle breezes put minds at ease?"

"Peters said you could stay in the cottage. Here, fill out this destination form. Put down Square Island by pedal tram and ferry boat. The tram leaves at 12:10." The clerk passed the form to Mildred through a tray that slid back and forth beneath the metal screen.

She filled out the form, signed and dated it. "There you are. I suppose I'm off to the summer home."

"It's for the best. You don't want to be in Pisstown if another Chaos breaks out."

"I certainly don't. And please get word to Peters. Tell him I'm going to Square Island and that if any of my grandchildren come home, they should join me there as soon as they are able."

"All right. Will do."

Having time to kill before the train came, Mildred ventured into Hooker Park and looked for a shade tree to nap under. There were stinker families picnicking under most of them, but a cluster of palmettos provided just enough shade for her to lie in and sleep for a few hours.

When she awoke, feeling rested, she looked up to see a young stinker female looking down at her with a curiosity. "How old are you? A hundred?"

"Oh, dear me, yes, a hundred and one at least."

The stinker said, "I've been shifted all over. I'm a third-stage now. I smell a little. My skin's drying out. I've been traveling with a couple of kindly Americans, the Camulettes. They're in the fourth stage. Come eat with us. We're right over there."

The Americans beckoned Mildred to join them at their table, where a charred imp head sat on a platter. "Come eat with us, there's plenty enough," Mrs. Camulette shouted.

When Mildred came to their table, Mr. Camulette said, "We know you. You're Mildred Balls."

"That's me," Mildred said.

"My name's Charity," the girl said.

Mr. Camulette broke into the imp's head with a hammer and chisel after scraping away some of the char. "Mrs. Balls, do you want some brains?"

"Yes, I'm starved."

"How about a Jake? We've got a whole pitcher mixed up."

"That would be nice. I'm parched, too."

Mrs. Camulette spooned a plate of brains for Mildred and poured her a glass of Jake. "We used to come here before we got infested. It's been wonderful having Charity with us. But we've decided to cash in soon, to have ourselves put down, so we'll have to part ways with her."

"I'll be an orphan again," Charity said.

Mildred was moved to sympathy. "I'll look after you. I've lost track of my own grandchildren. All the shifting, you know."

"I hate myself," Charity said, trying to shed a tear.

"She won't go near a mirror," Mrs. Camulette said.

"There are years left in her," Mildred said. "I could use some help when I get to Square Island. I'll be going there on the 12:10 tonight."

Charity's face brightened. "I'd like that very much."

Sampling a spoonful of brains, Mr. Camulette said, "It's a fortunate thing, running into someone as kind as you, and a person of means, too."

When the Square Island ferry departed that night, there was heavy chop across the Bum Bay Straits. The craft's oak ribs creaked and screamed its entire length as it turtled along at three knots, waiting for the night wind to catch its sails. Mildred and Charity clung to one another for balance at the railing and watched a fogbank slowly swallow Pisstown's yellow glow. "Without wind, or current," Mildred said, "we're like ants on a twig."

"My legs hurt," Charity said. "Look at them." She lifted her skirt to her knees.

Mildred cleaned her spectacles, then looked at Charity's leg with alarm. One of the leg muscles had popped through the skin. "Oh, dear, let's get a bandage on that." She found a clean bandana in her bag and tied the muscle back. "There, now. That will hold it in till we get to the cottage and sew you up."

"It doesn't hurt. It doesn't bleed. Why am I like this, Mildred?"

"Exactly why you're like this is impossible to explain. The one thing I know is, if you keep losing your parts, you'll blow away in the next strong wind. So, let's try to keep you together as much as we can."

"May I ask you a question?"

"Any time."

"How will the Camulettes put themselves down? They were so good to me."

"They'll go to a Templex and take a strong dose of willy, then have their hearts injected with formalin, stopping them almost immediately. After that the bodies are flash-dried, ground up and sold as fertilizer. It's one of the Reverend's ideas. Dust thou art to dust returneth, eventually, why not now? All that nonsense."

"I don't understand."

"Neither do I, dear. Only the Reverend understands."

At the Square Island Terminal, Mildred hired a Q-ped taxi. "To the Balls estate, please. And hurry. The girl has a tear in her leg."

"Yes, Miss, Miss Mildred. Long time, no see."

"I've been at Permanganate Island."

"We don't get much news out here. But I've got some for you. One of the Reverend's companies is mining teeth in your back pasture. Must have been a pretty big burial pit there once upon a time. There's talk of building a plant to process bone into meal there, too. Not to mention the potential for gas."

"That pasture is private property. This is a violation of the law."

"Not any more, Miss. The Reverend bought the Island. But don't worry. You're grandfathered in. You can continue to live on your property. You just can't do any mining. He owns everything under the topsoil, right to the core of the planet."

"Well, Charity," Mildred said, "At least we'll have a roof over our heads."

The clatter of the smoke-spewing, single-stroke, gel-burning engines used in teeth mining could be heard from the back meadow when Mildred and Charity entered the estate grounds, where a pall of exhaust smoke filled the air. "There was a time you could smell the sea from here," Mildred said.

It was difficult to see the main house at all, though a dim light shone in the window of the guest cottage and the moon cast enough light across the orchard to see that the persimmon trees were either dead or dying.

Mildred gasped. "Back then we always got ten or twelve bushels a year from those trees."

Charity said, "I'm like a tree. I hardly feel anything."

Hanging above the cottage entrance was a hand-scrawled sign that read, "Company Store & Diner."

Mildred feared the worst. "Someone's set up shop here, on my very private property. This is not something I'll stand for."

Inside the store, the candle light was dim, the air smoky. A layer of grime, crushed plaster, and tooth powder covered the once-varnished wooden floor. Shelves made of wooden crates had been nailed to the plaster walls. Mostly empty, they were stocked with a few jars of unguent, some bottles of Jake, and a box of starch bars.

"That used to be the dining room," Mildred said. "Every week of the summer there were Balls family dinners served. The big table is gone." Four overturned metal drums were serving as tables now. "This is a sad sight, Charity. Don't mind if I cry."

One corner of the room was partitioned by two quilts hanging from a rope and the scratching of a pen on paper could be heard. Mildred parted the quilts and looked in. A homely young woman sat writing at a desk. Without looking up, she said, "I'll be with you in a minute, as soon as I finish this letter."

"Excuse me, young lady, but—"

"I'm Katie. Katie Binder."

"Nice to meet you, Katie, but—"

"Wait, wait . . . I'm almost done." She had reached the concluding lines, which she spoke aloud. "I'm going to have to end this, Papa. Some customers have come in. Your loving daughter, Katie.'" The quilts parted and Katie came out. "All right, then. You folks hungry? Tonight we got eel. Pretty good catch this morning. They're fresh."

"Give me a Jake," Mildred said, sitting on a stool beside one of the drums, untying the bandana and carefully peeling it away from Charity's leg. "I don't see any necrosis. That's an encouraging sign. We'll put some unguent on it . . . I'd like a jar of that unguent, please."

"Coming right up. You two been shifted here?"

"No, no," Mildred said.

"I sure was," Katie said. "Used to be I had a sweet little business curing Jake and willy addicts out in Pisstown. Quite a money maker, too. And I get shifted here to wait tables, breakfast, lunch and dinner, for a stinking crew of teeth miners. Anyway, they already had supper and went back to work. We got a couple of eels left. That's all. I'll warm them up if you want."

"If I could taste food, and if I was hungry, I'd have one," Charity said.

Mildred placed five bucks on the drum. "The Jake will do for me."

Katie brought a warm Jake and a jar of unguent to the table. "So, what are you doing way out here on this stupid island?"

"That neglected mansion up there was my summer home for a hundred years."

"Really?"

"She's very, very old," Charity said.

"You're one of the Ballses that used to live here?"

"Mildred."

"Oh, yeah, they told me about you. They said you were good friends with the Reverend."

Mildred applied unguent to Charity's leg and re-tied the bandana. "You can't be friendly with someone who's killed your husband with a faulty parachute, but that's another story."

Charity rubbed her eyes with bent fingers. "I'm sleepy, Mildred. I want to go to bed." When she tried to open them, the lids were stuck closed. Mildred applied unguent to them with cautious strokes until they opened.

Katie put her hands on her squared-off hips. "Heck if I know where you two'll stay tonight. The miners live in shacks down by the mine. I have a cot in the back. You're welcome to get down on the floor here if you want. Or, there's a mule wagon coming through tonight, a big freighter. They haul kegs of teeth to Bum Bay. That's a heavy load, but they'll take on a couple of passengers for a few bucks. I wouldn't go back to Pisstown. It's still calm in Bum Bay, I hear."

"A mule wagon? There were never mules on the Island."

"They brought them in to work in the mines, for heavy pulling."

A little dribble of cadaverine made its way from Charity's nostril to her lip.

"Get me another Jake," Mildred said.

"Too bad the miners wrecked your property. They even poisoned the groundwater and killed all your persimmon trees. It's a shame. I must say, though, when the trees died, the imps ran off. They love persimmons, you know. They used to serve a good imp stew here."

"Yes, I remember. We tamed a few and kept them as pets for my precious grandchildren, who also loved persimmons."

Katie removed loaves of urpmeal bread from the pellet-stove oven and set them on the window sill to cool. "Here comes the freight wagon."

The mules drew the heavy wagon along the sandy road at a slow pace. Two Americans were aboard, one driving the mules, the other tightly clutching a carpetbag in his lap. The driver wore a wide-brimmed muleskin hat and a hand-sewn muleskin vest. A 20-caliber Sharps rifle lay at his feet. The passenger, who seemed wracked with pain, wore impskin boots and a tailored gray suit. He was unarmed.

"How's that back of yours, Mr. Harp?" the driver asked.

"I'm in unspeakable agony. I may as well be hanging on a cross."

"Probably worms got to your spine. Maybe you're infested."

"Not likely. I'm completely worm-free."

"What do you have in that bag you're hugging so hard?"

"That would be my business, Mr. Dewey."

"Well now, what are you, some kind of a snit?"

"My clothes, my toiletries, a tortoise shell comb. Nothing else."

"I'll bet. I'll just bet. It looks mighty heavy."

"I paid you five bucks for this ride. That should guarantee me some measure of privacy."

"We're stopping at Binder's for a while."

"Not for long, I hope. I'm in a hurry."

"Long enough for me to empty my bowels and fill my stomach."

Harp climbed down from the rig, still clutching the bag, wincing in pain with every movement of his back.

"Let me give you a hand with that, Ray."

Harp snatched it out of the driver's grasp. "No, thank you. I'll manage it myself."

"You've got something pretty precious in there, don't you? It's gold, isn't it? You've got a big brick of solid tooth gold in there, am I right?"

"Nothing of the kind."

"You know what they say about pure, porcelain-free tooth gold, don't you? To have it is to live in fear. To want it is to live in sorrow."

"I have nothing to fear, believe me."

Dewey entered the Binder store first, followed by a hobbled Harp, who had one hand on an aching hip and the other clutching the bag to his chest.

"Hello there, Howard Dewey," Katie said. "You haven't been through here in a while."

Dewey leaned his Sharps rifle against the wall. "Things were slow over at the mine, but now they hit a new vein, a big one. I'll be making regular runs from now on."

Harp sat beside one of the drums. "Two Jakes, please."

"What've you got for food, Katie girl?" Dewey chose the drum nearest his rifle to sit beside.

"Eels is all. And bread."

"All right, bring it on. I'm hungry enough to eat the ass end of a hydrophobic skunk."

Suddenly Katie was busy waiting tables and cooking eels.

Dewey tipped his hat to Mildred. "Evening, Ma'am."

"Good evening, sir. Katie tells me you sometimes take on passengers. We'd like to go to Bum Bay. I have a *pied a terre* there, with plenty room for myself and little Charity here. She's an orphan. She belongs to me now. I've given my word."

"I suppose I could put you in back, on top of the teeth. It'd be five bucks for you, three for the stinker."

Katie offered to warm an eel up for Harp. "No, thank you. My stomach is a little tub of acid. It was a hard ride."

"What you need to do," Mildred said, "is ball up some of that bread and drop it into your Jake."

"She's right," Dewey said, "Jake and bread'll do it."

Katie brought Harp a slice. In the process of balling the bread, he lost his grip on his bag and it fell to the floor, partially open. Dewey glanced down and saw the unmistakable glint of solid tooth gold.

"There it is, I knew it. This man has staked himself an illegal claim. No wonder he's got a sore back. He's been working his own private mine, in violation of every law on the books."

Katie picked up the bag and handed it to Harp. "Feels like about twenty pounds."

Dewey counted on his fingers. "That's what, on the Bum Bay market, that's a hundred bucks."

Harp said, "I was digging for potsherds. I found that brick." He held forth two open palms. "Do these look like the hands of a miner?"

Indeed, white and soft, with slender, delicate fingers, they were not the hands of anyone who'd done anything but light work. "I found it only a foot deep, under a dead persimmon tree, near the main house."

Dewey took up his rifle and pointed it at Harp's head. "Mr. Harp, sin has many tools but a lie is a handle that fits them all. Lying is a cursed and hateful vice. Now you ladies ought to turn around so you don't witness what I'm about to do."

"Let's be reasonable here," Harp said, shivering with fear, his aches forgotten.

"I'm going to take the law into my own hands, Mr. Harp. In the name of the Reverend, I'm about to march you outside, give you a pick and shovel to dig your own grave, then I'm going to unload this old Sharps right into your belly."

"I'm perfectly willing to share, even though I'm appalled at what I take to be outright armed robbery," Harp said.

"There's an element of finders keepers in all this, I have to admit," Mildred said. "But surely we should all have a share. It was mined from my estate, which entitles me to a share, and you, Mr. Dewey, will earn your third by taking us to Bum Bay."

"Me and Mr. Sharps, we'll keep you safe all the way. That I can promise."

Harp was somewhat calmed that Dewey had lowered the Sharps a few inches. "When we get to Bum Bay, we'll have it melted down and divided three ways."

"I'm sleepy all the time," Charity said, "but I never sleep much."

Katie led her to her cot. "There, honey, you lie down there and rest while I serve these people some supper."

When Dewey was full of eels and Jake, and had relieved himself in the ditch behind the store, the hour was late. All but Katie got aboard the freight wagon and hunkered down for the night-long ride. Mildred and Charity, both in a state of exhaustion, fell asleep quickly atop the sacks of teeth and didn't awaken until the wagon's wheels rolled noisily onto the wooden planks of the Bum Bay ferry and then stopped.

Dewey parted the canvas canopy at the back of the wagon, permitting Mildred and Charity to glimpse the pre-dawn sky and feel the chill of morning air. "You two better keep your voices down. There's a couple of Guards on board." He lifted Harp's bag into the wagon bed. "Hide the brick under one of those sacks. If they take a notion to look us over, and find this, it's the Purple Isle for all of us." He glanced away, then turned back, his face growing pale, his teeth set. "All quiet in there. Here come the Guards. Tuck that bar away."

Mildred acted quickly and the bar was out of sight, beneath a sack. Spreading her skirts, she sat on top of the sack and pulled Charity just next to her.

The Guards introduced themselves in a courteous and respectful manner as D.J. Purgeth, who wanted to be called Sasha, and D. St. Dizier, of the Reverend's Hookerite Guard.

"Good morning, people," Purgeth said. "Are we going to Bum Bay?"

"That was our intention," Mildred said. "My property has been appropriated. We have nowhere to stay on the Island."

"Who's the stinker?"

"I'm Charity. I'm only thirteen but I look a hundred. Isn't that funny?"

"I'm overcome with laughter," St. Dizier said, unzipping his tunic to reveal a spanking paddle affixed to his belt. "This paddle is made of hedge-apple wood."

"Sometimes known as bow d'arc," Purgeth added.

"No wood is stronger," St. Dizier said.

"With the notable exception of ironwood," interjected Purgeth.

"Yes, that's true, and these little spikes are intended to leave a bottom fairly bloody, even through the clothing," St. Dizier explained.

Dewey spoke up. "I'm just hauling teeth to Bum Bay. I've got all my papers, all my permits, all my licenses."

"Who is that person sitting up front, the one in the suit?"

"He says his name is Harp."

"Ask him to step down here. We need to have a confab . . . . Who's the old woman?"

"She says she's Mildred Balls."

"That's right, I am Mildred."

Harp climbed down and joined the gathering. "Have we done something wrong? I'm in unspeakable pain and in something of a hurry to get home for a long rest."

St. Dizier opened his tunic again and Harp saw the paddle, then Purgeth opened his, exposing an inside pocket stuffed with clean rags and another holding a bottle of liniment.

"I know you two," Harp said. "Purgeth and St. Dizier. The famous French spanking team. I've been to one of your shows."

"He remembers us," Purgeth said.

"Do you remember us, Mildred? What about you, Dewey?"

No answer came from either.

"Get out of the wagon, Miss Stinker. We're going to give these people a demonstration."

Charity clambered out of the wagon bed.

St. Dizier said, "My paddle has a hundred and one spikes. I'll give her two or three swats and we'll see the damage it can do."

"I'm ready with the liniment and rags." Purgeth held them out.

"Step out there in the open, Charity girl. Take down your skirt and your underdrawers."

By now, a small crowd of ferry passengers had gathered to watch.

"Don't worry, Mrs. Balls. It won't hurt." Charity raised her skirt. "I don't wear underdrawers. They stick to my skin. I wear skirts, so I can get air." She bent over.

St. Dizier slammed her bottom with his paddle three times in quick succession. The third blow knocked her off her feet. There was little bleeding, but quite a bit of torn and punctured flesh.

"That was fun," Charity giggled. "I think I felt something. A tiny, tiny little hurt. Can we do it again?"

"Sorry, girl," Purgeth said, "we've got fares to collect. Other wagons to inspect. You people go about your business."

The ferry's bell rang and the lumbering craft moved slowly away from the dock and across the gloomy straits without incident in just under twelve hours.

On landing at Witchy Toe, a small settlement on the West shore, Dewey drove the wagon off the ferry and to a roadblock for a cursory inspection by a Guard.

"Hey, there, Dewy. What's your load?"

"Teeth is all. They struck a new vein. I'm wore out. My mules are wore out. How much to let me pass?"

"Ten'll do."

"Here you go." Dewey handed him a ten.

"How far to Bum Bay?" Harp asked. "I'm in great pain, almost unbearable."

"It's not how far," the Guard snapped, "it's how long. In a rig like that you'll be four or five days getting there. You have to cross the Indiana Prairie, which, if you read the papers, is infested with rabid imps and pocked with the holes they live in. It's dangerous ground and the going is rough. You can hold a jar of urpmilk in your lap and make starch in about a half a mile."

"That ain't no fun," Dewey said, "even for somebody with a steel spine like me."

The wagon headed down Witchy Toe's main street and turned into an alley, passing a small crowd of men standing over a fallen stinker. Two of the onlookers, Major Peppard and Private Ratoncito, were in Guard uniforms. The Major wore thick-lensed eyeglasses and stood head-and-shoulders taller than his diminutive partner. Another onlooker, in a black suit, appeared to be a mortician. Shortly, a woman joined the group with a sketchpad and began sketching the stinker. "What stage?" she asked the Major. "Fourth?"

"Late fourth. He's been lying here three weeks, maybe five. The imps've been coming into town at night to feed on him. We're thinking we'll go on ahead with the burial tomorrow."

In preparation for casting a plaster likeness, the mortician applied hot beeswax to the stinker's face while an assistant stirred plaster into a pail of water with a wooden stave.

Dewey obeyed Private Ratoncito's signal and reined in the mules. For the first time in many hours, Mildred and Charity were able to part the canvas and look out. "It's nice to breathe fresh air," Mildred said. "Those teeth have a distinctive odor, like a stinker."

"I don't breathe any more," Charity sighed. "Or smell either."

The tall Guard tipped his hat. "Morning, all. Hello, Dewey."

"Hey, there, Major Peppard, Private Ratoncito. Got a load of teeth here and three passengers. How much?"

"Where you going?"

"Bum Bay."

"Let's say ten bucks."

Dewey handed down the money to Private Ratoncito. "Looks like one of your wheels is loose, Dewey. Better get on down to the blacksmith's. You don't want a broken spoke out there on the prairie."

Dewey spit cotton. "I'll be damned if bad luck don't follow me like my shadow. I guess I'll head over there right now."

Though the mules were dripping perspiration and foaming at their mouths, Dewey whipped them on. The wagon continued along the alley a few blocks to the Tooth Gold Exchange, pulling up to the loading dock at the rear.

As the sacks were being unloaded, Mildred and Charity availed themselves of a nearby latrine. "I do pass gas sometimes," Charity said, sitting on the hole beside Mildred. "But nothing solid ever comes." She stood and spit three teeth into the hole. "I don't need those anymore."

"Poor, girl," Mildred said. "Poor, poor girl."

When the wagon was empty and Dewey had collected a hundred bucks, the party continued to the blacksmith's, who was forging a part for a strange-looking wagon parked behind the shop. It had the general shape of a boat, with two wooden masts and light, thin wheels twelve feet in diameter.

The blacksmith rested his hammer on the anvil. "What can I do for you, Dewey?"

"What in tarnation kind of wagon is that out back?"

"That there is a wind wagon, my friend, made special for Reverend Hooker. You run them sails up, she'll roll over the

149

prairie like a ship on water. I'm forging her brand right now before I burn it into the stern." He grasped the branding iron with his long-handled pliers and lifted it from the coals.

Charity said, "That spells RH."

"That's right, little stinker girl," the smithy said, "it stands for Reverend Hooker."

As the blacksmith burned the RH brand into the still-green wood of the wagon's stern, sweet-smelling wisps of smoke drifted into the shop. "The Reverend's people will be down here in a few days to pick it up and sail it across the prairie."

Dewey was growing impatient. "I've got a loose wheel and a cracked spoke. And I've got a brick of tooth gold I want you to melt down and divvy up three ways. So hurry up."

"Soon's I finish here, I'll fix that wheel for you. It's about to fall off. You won't get a mile out of her. Can't melt your gold, though."

"And why is that? You got all the tools, you got a hot-as-hell fire. What else do you need?"

"You been out on that Island too long, friend. Hooker's declared that tooth gold possession is illegal. You get caught with it, you're going to be living on Permanganate the rest of your life. I'd go dig a hole and bury it if I was you. Maybe come back in a few years. On the other hand, if you want to be sure you don't get caught, leave it with me and I'll see about putting it under some dirt for digging up later."

"That is a heavy blow to the enterprise," Harp said.

"He's lying," Dewey said, snatching the blacksmith's hammer and handing it to Harp. "Here, hit him on the head with it, hard, when I tell you. You know what they say? They say 'He who lives by the hammer will die by the anvil.'" He raised the Sharps and pointed it at the blacksmith's chest. "This man here, by the name of Harp, he's going to brain you. So get ready and make your peace."

"Why do you think he's lying?" Mildred asked. "Shouldn't we give him the benefit of the doubt?"

"Look at that ugly face. It's got liar written all over it. Talks out the side of his mouth, all the time blinking, nervous as pudding. He takes us for a pack of cretins. You think he would have buried that gold once we got on down the road? Don't be an idiot."

"Hold your horses," the blacksmith said. "Just to show I'm not lying, look here." He took them a ways down the alley, where a broadside was tacked to a barn door. "See there."

The broadside depicted a brick of tooth gold embossed with a skull and crossbones. The warning was:

DON'T GET CAUGHT
WITH ONE OF THESE.

"It seems very clear to me," Mildred said.

"He could change his mind in a week," Harp said. "The price could triple when the law is rescinded, once he corners the market."

"True enough," the blacksmith said, "so if you want to take your chances, go on off with that brick and see what happens. And give my regards to Permanganate Island."

As they walked back to the blacksmith's shop, Dewey said to everyone, "Think about it this way. We keep the brick for a while and then we bury it out there on the prairie somewhere. When the law's been repealed, why we'll come on back and get it. This smithy's not entitled to even an ounce."

When they arrived at the shop, Dewey outlined a plan. "All right, we're gonna do the smart thing. We're taking the gold and we're taking that wind wagon, too." With the rifle barrel, he struck the blacksmith a sharp blow to his shoulder. The snap of bone was audible and the blacksmith fell backward, his head hitting the horn of the anvil, his numb hand dragging through the forge and flinging hot coals onto the hay-strewn mud floor. A fire began quickly, spreading outward in a perfect circle, setting the blacksmith's apron on fire.

"Everybody, on the Reverend's wagon!" Dewey shouted. "Let's get the hell on out of here."

"Look, that man is on fire," Charity said. "His face is bubbling."

Harp took a step toward the blacksmith. "Shouldn't we drag him out? He'll burn to death."

"Us, too, you moron," Dewey said.

Mildred and Harp nevertheless made an attempt to save the smithy. She took one of his feet, Harp the other, and they pulled until the boots came off, but managed to move him only a few feet before the fire drove them back.

Dewey looked up and down the street, then at his tired mules and broken spoke. He held his bandana in the air. "Luck's with us, folks. The wind's good and strong off the prairie. Everybody, let's push this wagon out and raise them sails."

Getting the wagon into the street and the sails raised took some doing. With only three adults and a weak stinker girl, it was a back-breaking push. But when the sails caught the wind, the wagon rolled along at a fair clip, leaving the black-smith and his shop in flames.

After two full days of a steady wind from the east, the wagon had made good progress. When it came to the ford at Bloody Creek, Dewey applied the brake and brought it to a slow stop, the front wheels axle-deep in water.

"Here we are, folks," Dewey said. "Once we cross the Bloody, we're in the prairie. If there's one, there's ten million imps that live there. We'll be running over them as we go. Figure we'll bury the brick out there somewhere, maybe in an imp hole. No mule driver'll ever take his animals where there's that many holes. They'd go lame in no time. A wind wagon's got that advantage, no mules attached."

The Guard and his deputy had stood by and watched the blacksmith's and the adjacent livery burn to the ground.

"Sure did go up fast," Ratoncito said.

"Dry wood, I guess," Peppard said, using a long, branched stick to roll the smoldering blacksmith out of the ashes. "His body's all asizzle. You hear it, Ratoncito?"

"I hear it."

"Smells like bacon, don't it? You ever had bacon?"

"Never did. Couldn't get it. Big shortages all the time."

"When the Reverend gets his re-meating imps to market, there'll be all we can eat all the time."

"Looking forward, Major. Looking forward to that day."

"Well, all right. There's Dewey's wagon and his mules. Now where's Dewey and his passengers?"

"What do you suppose happened to that wind wagon, Major? You think it burned up?"

"Most likely Dewey and company took it and went. They knocked that poor smithy out, set the place on fire and sailed off in the Reverend's own wagon."

"I 'spect we better go on after them, whenever the wind quits. Go get the artist and the mortician. We've got to put a notice in the paper and get the smithy and the stinker buried before we run out of sunlight."

When the wind died that evening, Peppard and Ratoncito were able to follow the wagon's tracks to the edge of Bloody Creek on a fast Q-ped. Within sight was an abandoned farmstead that consisted of a small sod house, a falling-down barn, a well, a privy and an old windmill. There were the dead remains of a persimmon orchard, a fallow garden and a dusty scarecrow.

The two Guards dismounted the Q-ped and crept toward the house. In the stillness of the morning they could hear snoring inside.

"They're sleeping," Peppard whispered.

"I'm not," Charity said. She was sitting on a wooden bench outside the front door, hidden in the shadows. "I get nightmares." She was holding the brick of tooth gold in her lap, stroking it.

"Quiet down, you," Peppard whispered. "We're fixing to make some arrests here and it'll be a damned sight easier if the perpetrators are asleep."

"What the hell's that she's got?"

"Lord God if it ain't a brick o' tooth gold."

"Where'd you get that?"

"Isn't it pretty?"

Ratoncito pointed his firearm at her and wiggled it. "Shoo! Go on! Git lost! Put down that gold and go."

"I'm with Mrs. Balls. She's taking care of me."

"Honey pie. You're on your own now. Follow them wagon tracks back to town. Go to the Templex. They'll take care of you. Walk due east, where the sun comes up."

Charity looked directly into the sun without squinting. "That way?"

"Yep."

"All right, then." She walked past the well, past the barn, and collapsed in the orchard.

"She went down, Major."

"It's no business of ours. The imps'll take care of her. We've got arrests to make. Possession of tooth gold, destruction of property, stealing the Reverend's wagon and who knows what all else."

One, then two imps left their wallows on the banks of Bloody Creek and stationed themselves in the shade of the barn. They remained still momentarily, making their final calculations before venturing out to feed on Charity.

"Looky there," Ratoncito said, aiming his finger at one of the imps pulling flesh from the stinker's abdomen.

"Our friends are hungry today," Peppard said. "Now, let's go on in there and give them sons of bitches a rude awakening."

When the two Guards entered the house, they found Mildred sleeping on a bare mattress, Dewey and Harp on the floor.

"Rise and shine," Peppard said, holding up the gold bar. "We've all got a date with the wig."

Dewey raised his Sharps and tried to curl his sleep-numbed finger around the trigger. But Peppard and Ratoncito stopped him short with eight shots to the body and head.

Harp sat up, terrified.

Peppard said, "We're taking you in for possession of tooth gold and for malignant neglect in the death of the blacksmith. And we've got a stolen wagon, destruction of property, and arson. State your name. Who's that old woman?"

"I'm Ray Harp. That's Mildred Balls. It's her gold, not mine. I'm an innocent party in all this. I was just a passenger."

The Major stepped closer to Mildred. "She's a damned deep sleeper, wouldn't you say?"

Harp clasped his hands behind his back. "She's very tired. We're all very tired. A lot of sleep was lost."

Ratoncito went closer, touched her forehead. "She's stone cold dead, Major." He placed his hand near her mouth. "I don't feel no breath, neither."

"Well, Mr. Harp, looks like we'll be taking you in all by your lonesome," Peppard said, rocking back and forth on his boot heels. "But first, I want you to give that old dead woman a kiss, right there on them lips. Don't be ascared."

"Not on the lips. I'll just give her a little peck on the cheek."

Peppard raised his weapon and cocked it. "You heard what I said. Ratoncito, what did I just say?"

"You said for him to give that poor dead woman a decent kiss."

"On the lips."

"Yeah, you said that."

"Get to it, Harp. We got a hard ride back to town."

"Isn't kissing prohibited? What if she's infested?"

"We'll all get 'em sooner or later. Eventually, why not now. Ain't that what the Reverend says?"

Harp bent over slowly and lightly touched his lips to Mildred's, which were far colder than he expected they would be, so cold that his head snapped back in reaction.

"Well," Peppard said, "let's get on back now. We'll leave these two for the critters."

Ratoncito snapped a pair of cuffs onto Harp's wrists.

Eleven.

There is rising demand among Hookerites for the construction of a cinderblock wall, thirty feet high, stretching from Indian Apple to Bum Bay, a distance estimated to be one thousand miles. "We want a community we can call our own," said a spokesperson representing the group. There are more stinkers now, the group believes, than fully living persons. "Many Hookerites," the Reverend recently observed, "are angry when they read the City Moon *and are told the same tiring lie, that there are more of us, the uninfested, than the cumulative sum of stinkers."*

As evidence of the growing problem, Hookerites cite news accounts of American settler populations dwindling before the influx of stinker immigration to the Fertile Crescent. According to recent investigations, stinkers in the area now number some sixteen thousand. Because the Crescent is the most luxuriantly rich and abundant land mass on earth, and thusfar relatively parasite-free, widespread infestation there could bring Chaos to a land where peace, prosperity and order were the rule.

A stinker widow in one of the bailiwicks went into business making her own pure imp sausages, which she served to neighbors on an urpmeal bun. She had learned how to make sausages when she worked at Zeus

Bologna Company. Before her husband was put down, he had built her a screened-in lean-to off the side of their trailer. It wasn't visible from Dunvant Road, and that's just the way the widow wanted it. She wasn't as clean or as careful as required by ordinance. There were worn gears in her grinder, which indirectly caused some tooth breakage when customers bit down on a piece of bone.

The widow was in violation of at least ten meat sanitation laws. She was ordered to stop production. "But people in the bailiwick depend on my sausages," she told the City Moon. "They send their kids over whenever I've got a batch ready. And they always know when that is because I hang a fresh-made sausage on my clothesline. They come running over with their little sacks and fill them full for a buck or two. They take them home and the family lives off them the rest of the week."

For as long as they could, neighbors learned to ignore the putrid smell that rose up off the meat in the summer months. It was kept sitting in an open tub, fly-covered piles of it, wormy and ripe. When a number of children took to their beds with taut, rounded bellies full of parasites, and one nearly died, the neighbors' complaints were given a hearing and the widow was ordered to cease the production and distribution of her tainted sausages. Ignoring the intent of the order, she simply began making the sausages at night after the air cooled down.

But she used gel cans for light, which brought bugs around by the hundreds and they often dropped into her meat and urpmeal mix. Still, hungry for meat, the children came. And again, they were taken sick. After repeated warnings from wigs in that jurisdiction, the widow's sausage-making continued until, weeks later, two Guards came to her trailer one evening *and exercised a warrant by standing her up against the side of her trailer and shooting her in the back of the head.*

It's the latest fad among third-stagers. You see them wearing canvas suits, coiled in rings of breathing apparatus, bobbing belly-up in the canals like poisoned fish. They tangle in water hyacinth, which strangles the canals every summer, then free themselves and float on, city to city. The afternoon sun returns blinding spikes from their goggles, scaring children and animals along the bank. On average, every summer, just under a hundred and fifty of these aquatic stinkers are eviscerated by hagfish.

News from the Permanganate Parasite Facility is that a component of the venom of the humble fiddleback spider has been shown to be a potent anti-parasitic. Several cases of spontaneous expulsion of the parasite have been reported and many of those confined on the Island are being released. Patients there had been kept in isolation to prevent the spread of infestation. In the end it proved not to be the isolation that halted the spread, but the presence of the reclusive fiddleback in many of the Island's remote living quarters.

A star is dead here, requiescat in pace. *Mitsuguro Bando, noted Kabuki actor, has died of hagfish poisoning at a restaurant in Pisstown. After his performance at the Flickerama, he dined with fans on roasted hagfish at the Palace Orienta. Upon remarking about particularly tasty hag, he suddenly collapsed, his cheeks engorged and pathologically distended.*

Bando's body, once preserved, will be kept in a curb stand made of opalescent material and illuminated by concealed lamps. During the day the stand will look like any ordinary glass structure, but when darkness comes the lamps will be turned on and the famous actor will be bathed in a ghostly, fluid light.

Once known as the Iron Duke for his ability to eat metal, glass, and stone, Wallace Hooker will announce his retirement from that practice at the Bones Jangle tavern Tuesday night. It was a nearly deadly meal that hastened his decision, he revealed in today's City Moon. *During a public demonstration at the Gons Hotel, he dined on imp brains until the kitchen was out of them, then ate his plate, his drinking glass, and coffee cup with saucer. After eating the tablecloth, he sucked twenty starch bars through a napkin. Then he went downtown, entered an antiquary shop and took bites from a tin sitz bath. "On a butcher's scale," Wallace said, "My stomach would have weighed fifty pounds. I had gone too far."*

William Parker Yockey's life has been cut tragically short by a hagfish attack. Vacationing on Square Island, Yockey was asleep on a hammock hung between two posts near the water's edge when what is suspected to have been a hagfish wormed its way out of the water at high tide and attached its tentacled mouth around Yockey's navel, extruded its horned tongue, macerated the muscle, then sucked out enough of Yockey's vitals to kill him.

Somehow the hagfish discharged a great heat in the process, such that there was nothing left of the shrubbery but a burned circle where the two struggled. This latest attack comes as a surprise to marine scientists, who previously stated that the hagfish would never enter the canal system. Now it is feared they will propagate on the slimy bottom, filling their bellies with nutrient-laden sludge.

Such memories of the first big Chaos. Confined to our Hyberhomes, often ten or twelve to a ten-by-ten space, we passed the time making up games to play. There was no room to move, or to scuffle and fight. We became well-organized and decided it was good to stay calm, to make the air easier to breathe. Some of us stood, while others slept, sitting with their arms around their knees and pulling them toward their chests.

Some of us formed a dream club. Before going to sleep we planned to meet at specific dream locations. After a few nights we began to recognize in common a shadowy, poorly dressed figure standing in the shadows of our dreamscapes. We all called him Dewey and we knew that he had come to threaten the peace and privacy of our sleeping world. Reasoning that he would feel no pain, we agreed to murder Dewey during the next round of dreams. We would meet at the Impeteria in Pisstown. Dewey would be there, waiting to haunt and taunt us without let-up. He could brandish a shiv in our faces or spit on our dream shoes. We never knew what to expect.

There were nine of us dreaming that night. Dewey little suspected he would be facing organized, hostile dream bodies, and when he did, he melted away like a candle. We had killed a dream figure by simply wishing it, not as an individual, but as a group. The solitary dreamer has little power. It takes a group to have any influence in the dream world.

Cora Fry Hooker, pretty nineteen-year-old niece of Reverend Hooker and daughter of Wallace, was found dead in a water trough at her father's home early Sunday morning. Her slender throat had been slashed ear to ear, and her left wrist showed gashes, but the Reverend's physicians stated the death was due to drowning. Cora was to be married at eight o'clock that morning to a prominent Pisstown merchant.

The young woman had been in the best of spirits Saturday night and had gone to bed at her usual time. The household slept and knew nothing of the tragedy until the body was found. In the parlor of the home, the proposed wedding room, the funeral was held this afternoon. Cora's shroud was her trousseau. Saying he was despondent, the would-be groom declined to comment.

Madeleine Mott, noted stinker artist, has survived a near-fatal, self-inflicted wound. She did it among a group of laughing children with whom she had been playing in Hooker Park last evening. The game was bargello, the object to kick the inflated bladder of a hagfish toward and across a predetermined goal line. In the pitch of darkness and without warning she pulled a pocket pistol, and, before her meaning could be understood by her playmates, discharged a bullet into her temple. Taken to the Pasteur Clinic, where a surgeon excised the spent lead, Miss Mott was back at her easel in a matter of days, content to be alive.

Shifted back to Bum Bay, to mate with one Carleton Manson, Ophelia traveled by pedal tram over the monotonous stretch of scrubland with only three or four outposts along the way. It took two full days for her to get there.

Before the introduction of the Q-ped and pedal tram, shiftees made the journey on the backs of prairie imps culled
from wild herds. They would not accept a saddle and were
impossible to control, wanting always to go their own way.
Before the rider knew it, an imp would have gone a hundred miles in the wrong direction.

On arrival, however, the imp would be slaughtered,
dressed, smoked, preserved in salt, and eaten on holidays
for seasons to come. On one well-documented occasion,
new arrivals were instructed to bring their imps to the
abattoir without delay. It seemed the ice-house had been
struck by lightning. All the winter's ice, cut in blocks from
the frozen Canal, packed in hay and stored there, had
melted. It was important now that all meat be smoked and
salted as soon as possible. After the long trip, the imps were
trim and the meat light. Slaughtering and dressing was a
relatively easy and quick affair. Some of the imps were so
exhausted they entered the chute that led to the killing floor
contentedly, even briskly. Now, with the wild prairie imp in
danger of extinction, Q-peds and trams are used exclusively,
but fresh meat is a rarity.

Midway to Bum Bay was the Witching Well, a must-see for
passing shiftees. The well, nested at the bottom of a great
land-subsidence, was about eighty rods across and said to
be bottomless. The water was black and very sour to the
taste. The ground sloped at a low angle up from the well
to the flat table-land above where hundreds of imps rooted
for grubs.

"That's the Reverend's imp farm up there," a fellow
shiftee informed Ophelia. "Lots of experiments going
on. I read in the *City Moon* that they've developed one
that can give meat without dying. You can cut off all the
steaks and ham you want. The next day, there they are,
whole again. I've eaten enough starch to keep a laundry

in business. Some bloody meat would be a welcome change."

"I would agree," Ophelia said. "I like starch well enough, but somehow it doesn't fully satisfy."

Ophelia arrived in Bum Bay on the warmest day of the year and was put to work within hours at the hair mill, where imp tails and manes were dried, ground into a fine powder, mixed with urpglue and run through machines that spun out artificial hair for use in the doll and mannequin trade. Because the repetitive actions of her single daily task, tying the hair into small bales and packing them in boxes, left her feeling anxiously energetic in the evenings, she began to follow the methods of Yogi Vithaldas. Before eating a light supper, she first performed the Nety Kriya, one of the six processes of purifying the body. She threaded a soft, wet cotton chord into her nostril, then steered it downward by way of the pharynx into her mouth. Then she grasped the end of the chord with tweezers, worked it back and forth and dislodged the night's accumulation of mucus. After that, it was time to clean her stomach by the process of Dhoti Kriya, which involved swallowing a long, wet piece of gauze, then rotating the stomach muscles. Again, it was to dislodge accumulated mucus, which came out along with the gauze. She drank a small glass of her urine every morning while it was still warm, and whenever she had to make a decision of any kind, she threw yarrow stalks out on the rug in her assigned quarters and consulted the I Ching. She kept time the Mayan way, in terms of two permutating cycles. One cycle consisted of eighteen twenty-day months. Its days had names like Pop, Ik, Akbal, Mac and Zac. The other cycle was called the Vague Year, with five dreaded, unlucky, days at the end, days that accumulated because the Mayan calendar had a slight variance with the solar year.

That winter Ophelia's mate appeared on the scene. She met him in Hooker Park.

"Ophelia Balls. Nice name," he said. "I'm Carleton Manson. I'm not a mater, you understand. But I sell suppositories, of my own prime jit."

Manson, a Hookerite, was a scruffy, suntanned little tramp with a knotted beard who smelled like urpflanz and whose eyes appeared to be upside down. He wanted to wholesale a hundred suppositories, his entire lot, for eighty bucks, a good price by Bum Bay standards.

As soon as she was in his presence, and could smell him, Ophelia sensed that Manson had hypnotic powers, that he might psychically influence her to the point of automatic obedience. In retrospect, she wished she hadn't, but she invited him up to her quarters to talk over the deal. She thought she could sell them to some of the females at the hair mill and make a decent profit. But she insisted that Manson leave the suppositories with her on faith. She had accumulated very few bucks at the time. He said he would leave half the lot and when he returned from a weekend doing other business in the Tektite Desert area, they would make the final bargain. Ophelia wondered why anyone would have business in the Tektite Desert, where the soil was ninety-five percent bone dust and the sun ogled all day.

Before leaving her quarters, Manson asked Ophelia if he could shower in her stall. She told him there was scarcely any trickle at all after noon, but that he could try his best. On his way to the shower stall, he said, "Hey, sister, it's a beautiful day. You want to try one of these?" He held out a shiny, gray ball of willywhack. "It's pure. Ten times normal strength in this tiny hunk. It's the best and the purest. Expect a complete cool-down of the endocrine system, low metabolism and sky-high energy. Never a dull or worrisome thought. I'll let you have it free. You can pay me from the profits to come."

She swallowed the willy and lay on her pallet. In a few moments, a wave of tranquility washed over her, body and spirit.

"Raise that dress, girlie, and pull those underdrawers down to your knees," Manson ordered.

When Ophelia complied, he inserted one of the suppositories, pushing it into her as far as he could with his thumb. Afterward he licked his fingers, smelled them, and grinned like a billy goat. "Pull up your drawers. I'm finished."

"I feel so good. Thank you."

Manson showered quickly and vacated the premises with the rest of his suppositories.

When Ophelia awoke the next morning and tried to squat over her slop jar, she blacked out, fell backward and spilled its contents over the floor. Her first thought was that the willy had slowed her metabolism far too much. She felt bodiless. She squirmed about the tiny room, trying to stand, covered in her own waste.

In three month's time, without a sign of menses, and with sickness every morning, she requested a meeting with her supervisor at the hair mill. The two talked as the supervisor made her rounds, checking the machinery, begging her shiftees to work harder. "We've got a warehouse full of dolls waiting for hair. Please, hurry."

When Ophelia came to the point of the meeting, she said, "The workers' handbook says we are to report to you if we become pregnant."

"That's a tricky predicament. I suggest you abort it. Was it by suppository?"

"Yes, I think so. Parts of it slid down my leg. It looked like wax."

"He offered you willy, am I right?"

"Yes, he did."

"He asked you to take down your unders."

"Yes."

"He made his deposit, then he was gone."

"He's never come back."

"We know that operator. Carlton Manson. Goes around planting his seed in the innocent and gullible. They're after him, the Guards, but they haven't caught him. I urge you again to abort that thing. He's fathered hundreds, all male, all ill-tempered hulks with inbred criminal tendencies."

"I'll think about it."

"Let me know tomorrow. We'll have it done in the clinic here. You'll be back at your machine in an hour. A physician is on call Mondays and Wednesdays. He'll get in there and take care of things for you."

That night, to help make her decision, Ophelia consulted the Reverend's *Field Guide*, randomly opening it with her eyes closed and pointing blindly to one of the entries, which was: "Thunder rolls beneath heaven—simple action and simple movement, in accord with the creative flux of the universe."

To her, the imbedded instruction was clear—to disregard shifting regulations and to leave Bum Bay for good. She would search for the right place to give birth, somewhere remote from the Chaos and despair of the shifting programs. She would pay no attention to her supervisor's warning about ill tempers and criminal propensities. She would do the simple thing, as the *Field Guide* had directed. And what could be simpler than packing a bag and walking away? Any direction would serve, wherever the roads took her.

The first outpost Ophelia came to, after a day and a half on the hot, dusty road, was a small stinker settlement called Harpstring. The thirty or forty stinkers who lived there slept in tents and survived primarily on commodities like starch bars and urpmeal from the Administration. Despite their low circumstances, the stinkers took Ophelia in. They were kindly, peace-loving, and happy to let her have the baby there. A former midwife in the group would assist with the delivery.

For the next few months Ophelia's pregnancy followed a normal course, with one exception—the fetus was unusually large, and the midwife confided to others that she anticipated a difficult passage. "She'll have to have it in a water bath," she said. "Plenty of rags and hot water will be on hand."

Ophelia spent all her time, night and day, lying in a rope harness. Beneath a covering tent, the apparatus hung from a rigid framework of wooden beams and had an open area in its hammock-like webbing for her bulging abdomen, should she wish to turn over. When she lay in this position, a bystander could appreciate the mass of the fetus. The midwife estimated its weight at that time to be eight or ten pounds.

When the time came, Ophelia's hair was tied into a top knot and she was made to lie in a shallow trough of heated water. A stinker was positioned at her head and another at her feet. Children stood by with bottles of vinegar. The midwife used a rag soaked with chloroform to render Ophelia unconscious. With stinkers standing around singing happy songs, the hours-long delivery produced an eleven-pound male infant with one foot that was twice the size of the other, flat, without bone structure and as round as a pie.

Confident that the malformed child would be in more responsible hands with the stinkers, Ophelia rested a few days, then, still a bit too weak to pedal very far, left her Q-ped behind for the stinkers, mounted a good riding imp and fled the settlement in the middle of the night.

The imp carried her overnight to the outskirts of Pisstown. There she would spend the night at a hostel, let the imp rest, and ride out again in the morning. Having left her *Field Guide* with the Harpstring stinkers, she was indecisive in trying to establish her next destination.

What course did she want to take? Which ones were even open to her? Would she be sent to Permanganate for leaving her post at Bum Bay? She asked herself these questions over and over again, often out loud. But no answers ever came. Perhaps it would be best to act randomly, without thought, reason, or care, to follow any impulse, no matter how whimsical or dangerous. In this scenario, death would have no dominion.

After tying her imp outside, she went to the check-in window at Hostel 210 on Industrial Road. The long ride, without food or water, had left her lightheaded and her walk was wobbly.

"You okay, lady?" the night-clerk asked.

"A room, please."

"With or without a view? Without's cheaper."

"Without, then."

"That will be one buck. Nice imp you got."

"She's a good ride."

"There's a stable around the corner. Ask for Mr. Hobson. Get your imp bedded down. Ring the buzzer three times when you get back. I'll let you in."

"Where can I get a Jake around here?"

"Next to Hobson's, a little place called the Flamingo. Two good shows tonight. Moldenke and the Doolittle girl."

"Oh, very good."

"That Jake'll be warm. Their cooler don't cool anymore. We ran out of ice two and a half years ago when the ice house burned down. Can't keep meat fresh, either.

It's all we can do to keep the flies off it and pick out the worms."

Ophelia's imp took her at a fast trot around the block to the stable, where she found Hobson sitting on a bench outside his livery, whittling.

"Help you, Miss?"

"I'd like to bed down this imp for the night."

"Only got one empty stall, the most pricey one. I'll throw in a bucket of groats and a pail of clean water. We got stud service here. You innarested?" He struck a match and lit a gel can on the ground. The dazzling blue flames gave off a minty odor.

"Can't you see, it's a gelding."

"Sorry, Miss. I'm half-blind. Doc says I'm infested. It starts in the eyes. Your vision gets lost."

"I'm so sorry to hear that. My grandmother was infested. I know what a trial it can be."

"Like I said, the stall's pricey, a buck and a half, but it's all I got. Tomorrow's Coward's Day and there's a lot of rough riders in town to give them heck."

"It costs more to lodge an imp in this town than it does a person."

"How about this. You take your imp in there and you feed it and water it and in the morning, you clean the stall. I'm getting too stiff to do much anymore. I'll cut the price to a buck."

Ophelia peeked into the stable. "Even in bad light I can see three or four empty stalls."

"Those are reserved for very important people. Reverend Hooker, for one. He's been known to ride into town with a couple of his Guards late at night, looking for fun."

"I'll pay now. It's getting late."

"You seem to be a good natured young lady, so I'll make you another offer. Back behind the stable here, I got a nearly new, seldom used, Q-ped that I'll trade you even for that imp of yours and of course there wouldn't be a charge for the stall."

Tired and anxious for a Jake, Ophelia agreed to have a look at the Q-ped in the morning light before making a final decision.

"She's a slick machine," Hobson said. "Belonged to my brother, Hobby. They sent him to Permanganate Island for something or other. I forgot what it was. Me, I can hardly pedal, stiff as I'm getting. Easier just to sit on an imp and go places that way."

Ophelia said good night to Hobson, who cautioned her to use the side entrance to the theater to avoid the crowd of shiftees waiting in line at the front. "It says no admittance, but don't pay that any mind. Go on in and down the stairs. The Flamingo's been running a one-man show lately. Calls himself Moldenke of the Afterworld. He claims he's been there and back. I think you'll like it."

"Thank you so much for your help."

Hobson nodded, blew out the gel can and sat in the dark. "You can't miss the theater," Ophelia heard him say. "It's the only place around with electric lights."

Ophelia could already see a dome of light beneath low clouds only a block or two away. Before ducking around to the side entrance, she stopped to look at the hundreds of shifted males standing in line, some of them fighting to keep their places. All were engaged in trading ideas about what mating techniques they planned to attempt. Some were showing their organs to others.

On the stairway down to the Flamingo, Ophelia smelled urpflanz cigars and heard light applause. She found an empty set of pedals and ordered a Jake. Moldenke hobbled onto the stage without introduction or preamble and told another tale of his post-life experience: "It wasn't too long before I was ordered to get aboard the *Amber Princess*, a vessel that seemed out of time. There were flying imps perched in the rigging, a flock of a hundred or more individuals. Their legs were thorny and chitinous and they had thickly-clawed, parrot-like feet. I had never seen such a being over here on this side. You felt a jolt of static electricity if you got too close to one that was laying an egg. Rather than make a nest, the imps launched their eggs from the rigging and watched them break apart on the deck.

"The ship's mates, whom we seldom saw above deck, wore clothing that was styleless, featureless and poorly made. If it wasn't gray, then it was brown, or black. They looked gaunt and sick and seemed perpetually wracked with pain. They had craggy, liver-spotted, misaligned faces, dotted with hairy moles.

"The *Princess* was a wooden ship. Whether it was propelled by wind and sails or a steam engine, I was never certain. I could hear a dull rumble from below, as if from boilers, yet I saw masts, rigging and rope above deck, though I never heard the flap of canvas, even on the windiest days.

"We workers slept in bags under the stars, sometimes awaking covered with frost. Some of us were struck in our sleep by falling imp eggs. When the ship made its ports of call, we combed beaches and shores for teeth. We were given sealskin bags to carry them in. We turned in our bags when we got back to the ship and the teeth were sent below decks for processing.

"Once I found a cluster of teeth as big as a cabbage. I dug it out of the sand and washed it in seawater. The surface was rough, scarred and barnacled, but when I held it up to the sun I could see sixty or seventy distinct teeth inside, uniform in size, and filled with gold. This was quite a puzzle, how this ovoid cluster of teeth had come to be cemented together by barnacles. As I was standing there mulling over what the answer might be, one of the ship's mates came along the beach and said, 'That's a valuable piece. Finders keepers. Listen to me. Don't go back to the ship. It belongs to you, kit and caboodle. Yet I feel I'll be owed something for not turning you in as a thief. We'll take that to a tooth cutter. What's inside is priceless, worth at least a hundred bucks.'

"Taking the mate's advice and allowing him to come along, I ventured on foot all the way across the Fertile Crescent to Bum Bay, where tooth cutters were abundant.

"The mate said, 'Your kind are always getting into trouble. My presence will be a mollifying influence if any monkey business gets started.'

"At the first cutter's shop we passed in Bum Bay, a master tooth cutter and two apprentices were at work polishing and cutting lapis. I lifted my bag to the countertop and the master cutter turned to the task of assessing my chunk of teeth, which he remarked was the biggest he'd ever seen. He broke it in half with a blunt, thick knife and a small pry bar. One tooth fell away from the rest. The cutter examined it. 'It looks like gold in there,' he said, 'but is it?' Gold is easily charged with electricity, so he rubbed it with a cloth and it quickly became so charged that a coin would jump six inches and cling to it. And a visible, painful spark struck the cutter's finger when he tried to pry the coin loose.

"There was another test. Tooth gold burns with a yellow flame and gives off a strong, resiny odor. The cutter shaved a tiny sliver of it with a surgeon's scalpel and held it over a candle. It flamed up bright yellow and gave off a strong odor. He was satisfied it was pure and genuine.

"The mate and I turned back across the Fertile Crescent and walked for five days, stopping only once at Jacob's Well, where a dredging operation was going on. The clam-shaped dredge, manipulated by a steam-powered crane, was raised from the murky depths and dumped a load of mud, bones and rotting vegetation on the shore. At the same time a man in deep-sea diving equipment surfaced with a basket of silver bracelets, jade necklaces, copper chisels, statuettes, other vessels and valuable ornaments.

"The mate said, 'You see, the settlers who once lived here believed that in order for something to be a sacrifice, it must be of great value. That's why so many small bones are dredged up. Sometimes they threw their children in.'

"'I suppose I have no choice, then,' I said, and threw the two halves of my tooth cluster into the water, much to the chagrin of the mate, who made every effort to throw me in, too, although I managed to hold my ground until he had calmed down."

Moldenke's knees began to buckle, his head to sag. "That's all, folks. I'm out of breath and hurting all over. Good night."

Ophelia applauded generously and finished her third Jake. Nodding with sleep, she decided it was time to return to the hostel. Her vacated pedal set was quickly claimed by a waiting customer. The Doolittle girl was to perform at twelve and the crowd was swelling.

On her way back to the hostel, Ophelia stopped by Hobson's to see if her imp might need more water. There were three other imps tied to the stable's posts and three rough riders talking, drinking Jake, and smoking urp-flanz.

"Evening Miss," one of them said. "You in town for Coward's Day?"

"No, just passing through. On my way home, just on the other side of Pisstown. I'll get there tomorrow."

"Where you stayin' the night?"

"At Hostel 210."

"We just saw a bunch of cowards checking in there. We'll give them yellowbacks heck in the morning. Don't be surprised if some eggs break on your window."

"I just stopped here to check on my imp. Is Mr. Hobson around?"

"Last time we saw him, he was walking an imp down to the abattoir. Reckon it might be yours. Said he'd made a deal, the imp for that Q-ped out back."

"There was no deal."

"Too late to do nothin' I 'spect. There's a meat shortage, you know. Imps ain't worth much on the hoof no more. You gotta guard them close."

Ophelia walked to the back of the stable. By moonlight, the Q-ped looked promising. There were no corroded welds, the chains were recently oiled, the tires solid and well-aired, the pedals barely worn. Perhaps the deal with Hobson was fair after all. She was getting tired of trying to satisfy the imp's needs as well as her own. A working Q-ped would be a lot less needy and would get her places much faster.

She rode the machine back to the hostel and rang the bell three times. The clerk opened a small portal in the door. "Oh, say, that's a nice Q-ped."

"Yes, I just took it in trade."

"What can I do for you?"

"My room. I have a room. I've been down at the Flamingo. The name is Ophelia."

"You a coward?"

"No."

"Sorry, we're full up. There's even some yellow-bellies sleeping on the roof."

"I've already registered. I was here earlier. I have a room reserved."

"Take a look at me, lady." He framed as much of his face as he could in the portal. "Do I look like the guy you talked to?"

"No, it was someone else."

"That's right. I just came on duty ten minutes ago. Whatever transpired between you and him is none of my business. He's gone home and gone to bed."

"Didn't he make a note of it? I paid him a buck."

"Tomorrow's C-Day, lady. Every room in town is taken. I'm so busy I could scream. Please, just move on. Get out of town. It won't be a pretty day tomorrow. It might get chaotic."

Resigned now to a night without sleep, Ophelia strapped herself into one of the Q-ped's pedal sets and rolled past the stable, past the darkened abattoir, the derelict ice house, and through a large encampment of cowards near a Hookerite shrine, before she broke into the open space and pedaled toward home.

Twelve.

Scientists say the stinker body is a mechanism made up of unnumbered parasites, in the brain, the nerves, the lowly bum-gut, the blood, and all major organs. It may be likened to a human city, where everyone is engaged in legitimate work—the journalists, the mule drivers, the starch vendors, the candlemakers, the pedal cab drivers and the physicians. Each one is a party to this end on his own behalf. The parasites that make up the stinker body work the same way. Their characteristics are discernable to a certain extent with the aid of a microscope. Of course it is possible there are parasites of life and life functions that we may not examine this way because of their extremely minute size, but they undoubtedly have the same work to perform. As a body, and in classes, they strive for the preservation of law and order within the stinker's bodily metropolis.

In parasites, the germ of generation never dies. Stinkers have parasites in them that are perhaps thousands of years old. That is why they are able to do things we never dreamed we could do, undergo changes and hardships we thought impossible.

With unemployment among third-stage stinkers at record levels, the Reverend has offered a plan: "A galvanic spark applied to the tissue of the hypothalamus, along with proper use of my Electric Belt and Suspensory Unit, will make them once again into productive workers. This I promise to all."

Parasites are sometimes slow of defense, but they are always on the defensive. Put someone who has become accustomed to hot weather in a cold zone and, until the parasites acclimate, that person will suffer all manner of quivering, chills and discomfort. But the parasites will finally accept the change. Put one who has lazed unproductively along in life in a position which requires hard work, such as mule driving, and that person's parasites will likewise rebel, then accept the altered condition.

The skin of an imp peels off the skull like birch bark. Should you cut open the head, you'd find its interior spaces filled with a spongelike material, a pale shade of yellow, as thin and dry as pre-edible paper. In the very center of this spongy mass sits the brain, which scientists say is not really a brain but a bio-botanic neural nexus capable only of rudimentary cognition.

Cooked any way at all, or raw, the taste of an imp brain has been compared to that of the legendary truffle. For some just the smell of one slackens their jaws. They flock to restaurants in defiance of the curfew, then come careening out, faces puffy and distended, giggling like children, filled to the gills on imp brain.

Stinker children on the dark side of Bum Bay have tented old City Moons *into dunce caps and are running the streets like pixies, firing their little spiked teetotums at the ankles of bystanders, often leaving lacerations, then poking them in the ribs with sticks, and in general annoying everyone. Many would like to see them taken away and sent to Permanganate. Adults, they say, have gone there for lesser offenses.*

There has been another scare in Pisstown's Hooker Park area. The residents were stirred and excited over incidents that have occurred in that portion of Pisstown. For the past weeks, knife-wielding stinkers in frightening costumes have made themselves conspicuous there, inspiring terror among women and children and in some instances putting male adults to precipitous flight. These visitations have become so numerous that Hookerite Guards have been sent to the site of the disturbances, but without unearthing the secret of the stinkers' hiding places.

It was reported today in the City Moon *that Carleton Manson, the notorious "father of thousands," was laid to rest in a Fertile Crescent pauper's field. It is estimated that during his thirteen-year insemination spree, Manson impregnated more than ten thousand females with his semen in suppository form. Approximately half of those pregnancies resulted in live births. It is not known how many have survived until today. Manson's death, it has been reported, was caused by a bursting of the abdomen brought on by a severe infestation of parasites. Manson once confessed that a genital deformity lay behind his criminal urges, the exact nature of which has never been disclosed.*

After a mile or two of walking, Roe came to a field of ripening urpflanz. His eyes blinked in the brilliant sun. He saw in the near distance a wooden machine as large as the largest house in Bum Bay. It rolled along on tall, steel wheels, ten of them, and moved at a fair clip across the field, harvesting grain and grasshoppers as it went. Underwear and rags hung along its wrought iron balconies. Stinkers stood by the third-story railing and waved at him. "Welcome, stranger," one of them shouted through a bullhorn. "Jump on as we pass. There's no way in hell to slow this thing down."

Through upper-level windows, Roe saw stinker males stacking sacks of grain in the attic space while stinker females made grasshopper pies in the galley below. In an even lower room, young first-stage males pedaled the heavy, cumbersome machine along. For each of the ten wheels, twenty or thirty pedalers were required to keep up momentum, even on ground that appeared to be as flat and featureless as a skillet.

Roe felt a sense of purpose here, a recognition that important experiences lay ahead. An inner voice revealed that a job awaited him and that he would have to get to a city of some size to find it.

Over glasses of Jake, a table of third-stage stinkers welcomed him aboard and saluted him with cries of, "Sharife!"

Roe repeated the cry without knowing what it meant, then gargled his Jake before swallowing, as the elders were doing.

"I'm Roe Balls. I just arrived. I don't know much about what goes on here."

"There's nothing much to know about."

"I have the sense that a job awaits me in a city around here. I think my experience may be in the service sector. I can't say for sure. Where is the nearest city?"

"That would be Pisstown. When we get to the end of this field, get off and head south by southwest."

A female brought him a slice of grasshopper pie, freshly made and piping hot.

"I don't have a compass, or a sense of direction. The terrain is unfamiliar."

"Look at the leaves, the way they blow. Prevailing winds are out of the north by northeast. The leaves will point southwest. Once you have been in the city and found your job, you will begin to see why we do things the way we do, how we make the best of what the Reverend gives us. We work with what we have."

Without warning, the great harvester bounced into and through a land-subsidence. The jolt made Roe reach out to catch his bottle of Jake before it tumbled off the table.

"These sinkholes give off gas," one of the stinkers said, "sometimes with a hellish odor and capable of killing. That one has weak gas. When we reach speed again, the wind will take it away."

The air filled with a sulfur-scented gas. Roe pinched his nose closed. Stinker females opened windows and placed stops under doors as the harvester sped along in front of a strong tailwind.

When the edge of the vast field approached, the pedalers slowed down as much as momentum would allow, giving Roe the opportunity to jump without breaking bones. He landed feet-first, then tumbled into a bramble thicket. By the time he made his way out, only his face and hands were cocklebur-free. A passerby would have thought he was wearing a suit of thorns.

It was a long, prickly walk to Pisstown, which was busy, noisy, and very congested. They were letting imps run in the streets and a festival was going on, a celebration of some kind. When Roe asked, he was told it was Coward's Day, an annual event to honor those who refused service during the first Chaos. Hundreds were in parade mode, males and females together, marching half-clothed up the boulevard with their backs painted yellow.

The mayor addressed the crowd by saying, "Cowards die many times before their death, you know, and the valiant only taste it once. In the stinker mind, cowards, having suffered most, deserve a day and a parade. As to the Chaos, not a soul remembered a thing about it. It was long gone and best forgotten. There is an old pharmacy in the Heritage Area, though, nicely preserved, which historians believe was the site of Hooker's arrest for stealing a tube of unguent cream."

When the speech was over and the awards were handed out, Roe went directly to the first employment office he saw and was immediately given a job serving Reverend Hooker, who, while his Templex underwent renovation, was staying at a seedy boarding house across the way as workers made perfunctory, lazy progress on the Templex.

Scaffolds had been erected and a few workers puttered about the premises. A pair of architects sat at a table under a persimmon tree, studying blueprints, sipping Jake and nibbling pickled roots. It wasn't a bombed-out look the Templex had, but one of neglect, of a plantation house gone to wrack and ruin.

In the early days Roe's duties began with giving Hooker his morning enema and seeing that he took his willy. Starching and ironing his shirts came next, then keeping his nails trimmed and polished, shaving, trimming his van Dyke and, if it was desired, masturbate him over the sink.

When Hooker learned of Roe's saw-playing gifts, he insisted on hearing it three or four times a day. "What a mournful sound it is," he observed. "It resonates with the soul."

On a typical morning, after playing his saw at Hooker's bedside to wake him, Roe would say. "I am very glad to serve you this morning. What would please you for breakfast, sir?"

Most often it would be a simple one of urpflanz tea, grasshopper pie, and an imp steak. Sometimes he would forget about all the shortages and request cocoa spiced with vanilla and marzipan, too. Roe would have to remind him. "It's the Chaos sir. Those sorts of things won't be coming over from the Crescent, or so they tell me."

"Listen to me, Roe. Out of the Chaos will come a future of abundance and joy. We'll be swimming in cocoa, choking on marzipan and singing praises to you know who."

"Yes, indeed, sir."

In his bathrobe, Hooker would open his day's first bottle of Jake and hobble unsteadily to the grimy window, crank it open, and air his first thought of the day, most often a complaint, a curse or a gripe. "When are they going to finish with that renovation, when I die and start stinking?"

When spring came, Hooker coated himself in scented oil to prevent sunburn and ventured out to his garden plot behind the hotel. Here he demonstrated to Roe the principle behind a National Socialist garden. "You see, you dig it in the shape of a swastika. Can you think of a better way to lay out a garden? Every part can easily be reached with a hoe, without having to step in any dirt."

Hooker's temporary office and quarters in the Tunney penthouse became a scene of remarkable squalor and disarray. Roe offered many times to bring in the cleaning crew and have the place cleaned, but Hooker stubbornly forbade it. "I own ten imp farms," he said each time. "I've learned the pleasure of wallowing."

There were stacks of newspapers rising from the floor in waist-high columns. Imp bones and Jake bottles were strewn about. One of the flags that flanked his desk was partially burned. The Reverend had set it ablaze one day with a cigar. Roe had put it out by urinating into a jar, then dousing the flames with it.

The windows were boarded over, the floor covered with newspapers. A five-gallon slop bucket sat in the corner with a cloud of blackflies buzzing over it. A large nail had been driven directly into the plaster wall to hold a roll of wiping paper, a rare and expensive commodity during a Chaos, always in short supply otherwise.

There were bullet holes in the wall, falling plaster, spider webs. The Reverend kept saying to Roe, "This is a big country. Its inhabitants have never lived in walled cities or had to defend themselves against warring princes in neighboring states. After the first Chaos this country was so sparsely populated that neighbors were something to be longed for and were not fenced out. A new face or new arrival was a cause for rejoicing."

Most mornings found Hooker passed out at his desk, looking sorrowfully un-Reverend-like, his head, arms and shoulders buried in the desktop clutter, a bottle of Jake sitting near his fisted hand. Day and night there was a light film of perspiration on his balding head. Even though he looked puffy and ill, he was never without a fat urpflanz cigar, hand-rolled, which he pinched between two fingers, held at a distance and never puffed on or brought near his lips. He let them burn until they were almost spent, then spat on the burning tip, or doused it in Jake, and ate the butt.

His hands were beat-up, dirty, average size, somewhat simian, the fingers unusually short, the nails unusually long, thick and dirty. As if playing a tiny piano, these fingers moved in time to music only he could hear.

What was left of his hair was wild, dirty and knotted. His flesh, tinged yellow, had broken out in rashes and welts. There was dried vomit down the front of his filthy, terrycloth robe, which bore on the pocket the seal of the Reverend. And around the desk were the sometimes fresh, sometimes old and crusted, results of his unpredictable and incontinent "accidents." He sometimes stepped in them and tracked feces everywhere. If there was enough water, he bathed once a week.

An irreversible neurological syndrome caused by the prolonged drinking of Jake afflicted him. Its characteristic features were involuntary movements of the face and mouth and of the forehead, eyebrows, cheeks, legs and arms. He frowned, blinked and grimaced. He smiled, pouted, puckered and smacked his lips. He clenched his teeth, bit his lip, and his tongue protruded unnaturally.

He said to Roe one day, "I'm going to put up an artificial moon. My scientists tell me it can be done. It will be a medically significant moon, intended to cleanse the atmosphere of airborne bacilli for all time."

"Fascinating," Roe said.

"I've always thought the moon was the source of the parasites. By some little-understood means, they made their way here. That will be at the heart of my next sermon."

"Exciting and informative," Roe said.

"One more promise I'll make to the people. Jake will sell for a buck a bottle and be standardized. The quality will improve dramatically."

"Standards are what we live by, sir."

"I feel I need an enema, Roe. I feel full."

"I'll warm up the bathroom right away, sir, and get the enema bag ready."

Once Roe had firmly inserted the hose, the Reverent sat on the pot and closed his eyes. "There, that's it, Roe. It's in well enough."

"Shall I leave you alone now, sir?"

"No. Don't leave. Let me sermonize a little. I'll tell you a story, a story with a lesson. In the days when all men were good, they had miraculous power. Lions, mountains, whales, jellyfish, hagfish, birds, rocks, clouds, seas, moved quietly from place to place, just as men ordered them at their whim and fancy. But the human race at last lost its miraculous powers through the laziness of a single man. He was a woodman in the Fertile Crescent. One morning he went into the forest to cut firewood for his master's hearth. He sawed and split all day, until he had a considerable stack of hickory and oak. Then he stood before the pile and said, 'Now, march off home!' The great bundle of wood at once got up and began to walk, and the woodman tramped on behind it. But he was a very lazy man. Now, why shouldn't I ride instead of galloping along this dusty road, he said to himself, and jumped up on the bundle of wood as it was walking in front of him and sat down on top of it. As soon as he did, the wood refused to go. The woodman got angry and began to strike it fiercely with his axe, all in vain. Still the wood refused to go. And from that time the human race had lost its power."

"That certainly explains everything I've ever wondered about, sir."

"You may clean me now."

"Yes, sir."

A scant month after the renovations were finished and Hooker returned to the Templex, he decided that he could no longer be seen in public. "I'm going to be a different man from now on. I'll assume another identity, a more satisfying one. I'll step out of my self for a while as actors are known to do. Even my nervous tics may disappear. Perhaps that is the answer. I will take it under advisement."

"Would you like me to draw you a warm bath, sir?" Roe asked that evening.

"Yes, and get me some willy and a Jake. Nothing warms me better."

"Only Jake, sir. That's all they're letting you have. No more willy."

Hooker lay in the warm tub for hours, drinking Jake and thinking up new policies, while Roe sat on the closed commode playing the saw and occasionally taking up a notepad and pencil.

"Take this down," Hooker said, sloshing Jake in his mouth. "I'm afraid if we send up a medical moon it will be too magnetic, that it will lift junk from junkyards."

"Got it, sir. Shall I soap your back?"

"Oh yes, by all means."

Roe knelt beside the tub and applied floating soap to a sponge. "Shall I go ahead and lance these boils while I'm at it?"

"Leave them alone. They come and go. It's not a bother. I like them."

"Yes, sir."

"I don't think I'm long for this office, Roe. I've lost control. Was it the shifting programs?"

"I think they're a shining success, sir. Look at me. Would I have been here with you otherwise?"

"Roe, boy," Hooker said one day, "You're as close to everyman as any man I've ever known. That's why I try out my ideas on you first."

"I'm honored, sir."

"Without periodic Chaos, a society like ours would surely fall into a slump. Don't you agree?"

"There's no doubt about it."

"I'm soon going to propose a five-year moratorium on all productive activity. We shut down the factories, we board up the banks. Commerce grinds to a halt. And out of all the resulting Chaos and suffering, maybe we'll come to some kind of agreement as to what's worth doing and what's not. I give you the example of the legendary old boll weevil. Any cotton farmer could have told you, the best way to get rid of weevils was to stop growing cotton for a few years."

"Solid logic, sir," Roe said, "almost geometrical in its simplicity. That's the kind of idea that can't be denied or aborted. I've got goose-bumps, frankly. I've heard of cotton, but I don't know much about it. I do know that my grandmother has a dress made of it. She showed it to me once. It was soft to the touch."

A month later, in the middle of an icy January, during a night of fitful sleep, Hooker encountered what he claimed was the ghost of a stinker. The frightening stranger was discovered in a clothes closet when Hooker decided he needed warmer bed clothes. Reaching in for his woolen pajamas, his fingers glided across a grizzled cheek and he nearly collapsed. He tried to call out for help but his voice box was paralyzed. As in a nightmare, his mouth merely shaped itself around the words but he couldn't speak them.

"Don't be afraid," the stinker said. "I'm Joseph Lovell, builder and owner of the building. I've lived here two hundred years tomorrow. I don't know where in the building I stay. It's a dim, damp place, perhaps the cellar. I don't know how I got into your closet. I may have been there for a decade. How would I know?"

Hooker closed the closet door and heard no more from Lovell the rest of the night and in the morning related the episode to Roe. "I tingled after meeting this Mr. Lovell. I'm still tingling all over. Like a mild current running under the skin. It's maddening."

In the days after Lovell's first appearance, Hooker's condition worsened. He didn't trust the ice they brought him from the kitchen. He suspected the staff of putting chemicals in the water. Arsenic, he thought, would explain why his stomach boiled like a vat of acid without relief, and why he was acquiring a greenish glow.

Roe recommended that an aquarium be placed in Hooker's oval office, filled with seaweed, urchins, a bubbling diver and a baby hagfish. It was an effort to keep him amused and therefore calm. But once the aquarium was installed, no further attention was paid to it. The water dried up and all the creatures died while Hooker watched with intermittent attention.

On a nocturnal visit to Hooker's bedroom, after using the toilet, Lovell said, "Excuse me, but the bowels of ghosts do move, despite the popular notion to the contrary, rather frequently as a matter of fact. But what's produced is just a squirt of ectoplasm and a little gas."

Hooker asked to be allowed a pet or two and he was given a mating pair of miniature imps. He named them Harvey and Marina. Harvey sickened and died fairly quickly and Marina ran off. "They were a fine pair," Hooker lamented to Roe. "I miss them a lot."

Later the two imps were found. First Harvey, when the Reverend fell against an office sofa, moving it a few feet and exposing the imp, long dead and completely desiccated. Hours later the same day Roe spotted Marina from his window. She was frolicking with a stinker child near the fountain.

Some mornings Hooker made a modest effort to look presentable, but usually managed to over-tonic his hair or put on a wrinkled suit. No one came to see him anyway. He had a model motor car on his desk and he liked to play with it. Lunch was always something he looked forward to. He was served a variety of things he called for, like skrada-kaka, marrow pudding, tanfy and friters, all favorites of his childhood.

"I'll stage my death," he whispered to Roe during an enema session. "Then I'll be spirited off to a hideaway in the Fertile Crescent where I will live out my days in a simple home of my own design. The public will forget me quickly. Word will go out that I'm ravaged by parasites. I'll linger until I fade from public consciousness, then I'll be laid to rest in a private ceremony. It would be an official death, not a real one. I'll be augmenting dull reality, giving it a mythical feel."

One night after hearing Hooker's screams, Roe found him nude in the bathroom, standing on his head, trying to pass a kidney stone. "I learned this trick from an old stinker," he wheezed.

When the stone failed to pass, Hooker's physicians were kind enough on that occasion to give him willy. The pain was greatly eased and the stone passed in his sleep. "Save it," he told Roe, "it may be a valuable relic some day."

Roe placed the stone in the pocket of his rags and promptly forgot the instruction. Some weeks later it would be pulled from the pocket unnoticed while he reached for a key to the china cabinet. It would roll along the floor and come to rest beneath the cabinet, never to be found or thought about again.

With scarcely a month remaining before his fatal disease was scheduled to strike, Hooker reminisced to Roe, "The people wanted a Reverend who could deceive enemies and charm friends, or vice versa. That was my public appeal. I had lain among the hopeless and desperate. I was a bum with panache, unshaven but dignified. Street-wise, blunt-talking, cynical, not happy, a long history of unemployment, a leader who'd spent time on the Purple Isle. That's what people were crying for. 'What you see is what you get' was my campaign slogan. I faced the public *au naturel.* I hung out my dirty laundry with pride, exorcised my demons in full public view. I humiliated myself for the common good. I got in trouble, I got arrested. I was always in the news. I said outrageous things. It was the politics of the actual. Now look at me. I'm all washed up."

Roe was trusted with getting the Reverend ready for travel. Arrangements had been made for the renowned pilot, Buster Knabenshue, to fly him to Bum Bay. From there he would get a ferry to the Crescent. It was thought unlikely he would be recognized, and if he were, he would be ignored.

"You may dispose of my things when I'm gone," he said to Roe, who heard the clink of cables and chains as Knabenshue's orbigator was tied to the Templex flagpole.

"I'd best get going," the Reverend said, "but I'll be back when the dust settles. You've been a good servant, Roe. I do hope your next shift is as fortuitous as this one. Goodbye."

"Goodbye, sir, and good health."

Roe's heartbeat quickened as Hooker dashed out to the flagpole with his luggage. Letting out a yodel, he belted himself into the lift harness and was hoisted up to the orbigator, where he threw his luggage into the aircraft's luggage bay and took one of the two remaining seats. "Very snazzy craft, Mr. Knabenshue," he said. "And so spacious."

The craft was propelled by a galvanic motor, steam vessel, and two balsa screws more than three yards in diameter. There was, in addition to the cockpit, a sleeping area with seven stacked cots and a fully equipped kitchenette. Mrs. Knabenshue baked bread and cakes as the orbigator flew. The aroma was enticing.

When the craft reached a good altitude, Knabenshue relaxed his controls and let it drift. The screws turned with remarkable quiet. The canvas wings stiffened and cut like table knives through the ozone, the metal ailerons rat-tatting like tin drums.

As the orbigator passed over a stinker refuge, Knabenshue said, "This is rich. Let's go down," and landed near a field. Some sort of fair was taking place. The stinkers were cooking nineteen thousand pounds of fattened imps over a great trench. They explained that the fire was started yesterday in fifty cords of ironwood and urpflanz brush, laid in a trench seven hundred feet long. A stinker barbecue artist was on the grounds to direct a corps of assistants in the stoking of the fire, so as to reduce the wood to the proper kind of coals.

The feast was to be given in honor of the birthday of the oldest stinker, Prester Jack, who established the first stinker settlement and ruled over it for a century and a half. It was called Arden. A herd of imps broke through the fence, legend has it, and ate all the corn. Famine ensued, until an imp was trapped in a burning barn and roasted. Prester Jack, they say, took the first bite. Then the others joined in eating the tasty meat. Thus the famine was ended.

A stinker docent took charge of Hooker and his party. "Look," he said, a thin arm thrust outward, the hand gloved in chamois, "There's no reason for you Yanks to be bored here. I

191

can take you to our amusement park. We have the Aerial Swing, Box Ball Alleys, Automatic Shooting Gallery, Palm Garden and Café, German Village, Roley Boley, Ice Cream Parlor, Airchairs, and the Mystic Mesh. If that isn't enough, we have games like policy and craps, poker and spades, whatever tickles you. And the well known Doolittle girl is appearing nightly."

The smoky air was filled with the scent of barbecue. As Hooker and company ate platters of meat and urpmeal bread, they were entertained by watching young stinker males attempting to mate with the Doolittle girl, who lay on a bed of grain sacks, in a gingham dress raised to the waist. With her vaginal opening illuminated by a gel can held close, those positioned for a clear view saw the pearly pink laminations of the complex organ exude a whitish lubricant just before the first male made his attempt with a clumsy, misdirected thrust that did not achieve full penetration.

Hooker said, "I could do it. I'm getting in line."

"No, no," said Knabenshue. "I don't like the look of the sky. We should fly out before the bad weather hits."

The party made for the orbigator and flew out of the area and above the coming storm. That evening, as the craft flew, Hooker and the Knabenshues passed the time playing hearts, liar's dice, and double solitaire. When that grew dull they amused one another with recitations of facts and figures. Hooker said, "Oysters lived in fluid that contained about one part salt to twenty-seven water. You could have raised them in your home."

Knabenshue said, "It has been frequently noted by orbigator pilots that the barking of an imp is always the last sound they are able to hear from the ground when they are ascending, even to an altitude of four miles."

Mrs. Knabenshue said, "Parasites can live for years in the carcasses of buried stinkers. Imps rooting through old lime pits have been infested. The parasites are brought up to the grass by worms."

A little before dawn, Hooker awoke, looked out the window, and saw the streetlamps of Pisstown. To the south was the royal blue glow of the National Canal. Schools of hagfish grazed like buffalo on the bottom. There were pedal wagons already making deliveries of urpmilk and urpmeal bread to the restaurants catering to *pain du perdue* enthusiasts. There was a Jake wagon piled with kegs, an American pedaling a waffle van and tooting a kazoo to attract a clientele.

Knabenshue set the orbigator down in Hooker Park, where the Chatterjee Brothers were putting on a twilight concert, plinking twin pianolas in the band shell. Hooker took a pedal cab directly to the Tunney Arms, booked a room and went out for supper at the Palace Orienta.

When he entered, kidneys sputtered on the grill, brains bubbled in hot fat and a cricket fiddled on a window sill. A husky young American male sitting at a back table drinking a cup of urpmeal, stared at him. The American's fingers tapered carrot-like from thick hilts to infantile points and one foot, shoeless, much larger than the other, rested inside a drawstring bag. The young man wore a shawl and a heavy coat, yet still shivered.

Hooker was shown to a small, two-seat table near the kitchen door.

"The special tonight is imp steak, Mr. Reverend, served on a bed of urpflanz sprouts," the waiter said.

"I'm sorry, but I was told no one around here would recognize me. You did."

"Frankly, sir, I didn't. That American who's waving at you. He told me who you were."

The young man raised a finger and forced a smile, gesturing in a way that indicated he wanted to sit with Hooker, who nodded in the affirmative. The American's progress to the table was remarkably slow. Every tiny step pained him greatly. Sensing this, and thinking the man might fall over and hurt himself, Hooker stood and gave him a shoulder to lean on.

"Thank you, sir. Thank you. It would be an honor to dine with a sitting Reverend."

Once situated at the table, the man spoke obliquely for a while about the origin of Pisstown. "The north-south and the east-west pedal trams go through here. It's a hub of gray-market trading in imp jowls, frozen heads, Jake powder, organ meat, imp pelts, anything anyone might want. And it's in the Fertile Crescent, so the weather is mild all year round."

"Yes," Hooker said. "I plan to retire in these parts."

"Despite all that, I feel sick unto death," the young man said. "My mother abandoned me a long time ago, left me with a band of nomadic stinkers and this horrible foot. Now I've got a bad case of parasites. Can you help me?"

"Yes, but how?"

"They say you have a license to kill."

"Not any longer. I've stepped down. I'm just a citizen, like everyone else."

"Please. Show a little mercy. There's only one way to cure what I have." From a pocket within the folds of his coat, the young man took a small-caliber pistol. "It would be a comfort to die at the hands of a great man like yourself."

"I'm very sorry, but I can't do that. They'd send me to Permanganate Island."

"I'll do it myself, then." He touched the barrel gently to his temple and fired. But because that shot failed to deaden his pain, he shot himself in the eye. Within a few moments, he fell lifeless to the floor.

Guards appeared on the scene, questioned other diners and the waiter, and made a swift arrest. The following morning Hooker was sentenced to ten years in the Permanganate Island prison for malignant neglect.

There were side-shifted innocents among the guilty at the prison facility, confined to their cells after curfew, but permitted to stroll along the violet beaches during the day. Owing to the toxicity of the sand, however, these strolls were limited to a hundred steps in one direction, then a hundred back. Otherwise, shiftees could wander about the greener central parts of the Island as they wished.

In his cell, Hooker had a gel can that sat on a tiny table near his cot and he used the black soot that collected on a stick held above its flame to do arithmetic problems on the wall, long numbers times other long numbers, the results divided by small fractions. Also he used soot to mark the days with streaks on the wall and to draw simple stick figures with perfectly round heads. The gel can's light was sometimes used, as well, to project shadow figures for amusement.

Standing on tiptoe he could see a high stone wall and a four-seat latrine. Prisoners lined up all day and night in the rain to use it, the red-tinged water running down their faces and off their hats like blood. Sometimes the rain stopped suddenly and when it did the sun baked the Island ferociously. Hooker stood in the potty line one day for three hours, forced by regulations to go naked. By the time he got relief, he was covered with blisters and his flesh burned red.

During year four he shaved his mustache, grew a goatee, and refused all nourishment for forty days. At the end of this period, Guards have testified, he was transparent. "If he stood before a candle," one said, "you could see the flame flicker behind him, and the outline of his spine."

Year five it never stopped raining and thundering outside. Violet-tinged water seeped through the prison wall and flooded Hooker's cell to a depth of six inches. When it receded, months later, his feet were deeply wrinkled, soft, stained a shade of purple and impossible to walk on for days.

Year six, prisoners were given haircuts. Hooker didn't want one. If you had long hair you could play with it. You could plait it, twirl it, wrap it around your head. It gave you more things to do with your time. So Hooker fought with the barber. He slammed him in the throat with his boot. When the barber yelled, the Guards came in. They slapped him around until they could no longer lift their arms.

Year seven Hooker shaved his head and face and sat cross-legged on the floor, carving tooth-shaped nuggets out of soap with a long thumbnail that he'd let grow for this very purpose. He made a drawstring pouch out of a bandana to keep his nuggets in. When he held it in his hand and imagined there was gold inside, he felt a childish glee.

Year eight he collected earwigs from the damp floor and put them up his nose and in his ear canals. He plugged his nostrils with soap and held his hands over his ears. Once he got used to them moving around in his head, trying to dig their way out, it became an addiction that ranked second only to masturbation.

When year nine came along, he grew a bushy mustache and lay on his cot in a state of suspended animation. It was the year his legs began to stiffen and grow numb. He remembered almost nothing of the seasons other than the sunny summer day when he watched a pair of grasshoppers mate on the bars of his window.

Ten was a snowy year, dedicated to counting the days until his release. He stiffened even further as time passed and could sleep only by kneeling on all fours. When the day of his release arrived, he was issued a suit, a tie, a big hat, a sack of starch bars, a small wog of willy, a morning edition of the *City Moon*, and a ticket for the ferry to Bum Bay.

"Look here, Hooker," the Guard said, tapping the rolled-up paper. "The Pisstown Chaos is over. People are finding work. Anywhere you go, there's a job to do."

"Thank you for that tip," the Reverend said, tucking the paper under his arm. "I do like to watch people work. It fascinates me."

The Bum Bay ferry arrived at Permanganate Harbor a few minutes ahead of schedule. With the help of a Guard, Hooker climbed stiffly aboard, chose an aisle seat and strapped his feet into a set of pedals.

The End

David Ohle's novel, *Motorman*, was published by Alfred A. Knopf in 1972 and re-released by 3rd Bed Press in 2004 with an introduction by Ben Marcus. Its sequel, *The Age of Sinatra*, was published by Soft Skull in 2004. He has edited two non-fiction books, *Cows are Freaky When They Look at You: An Oral History of the Kaw Valley Hemp Pickers* (Watermark Press, 1991) and *Cursed From Birth: the Short, Unhappy Life of William S. Burroughs, Jr.* (Soft Skull, 2006). His short fiction has appeared in *Harper's*, *Esquire*, the *Paris Review*, *TriQuarterly*, the *Missouri Review*, the *Pushcart Prize* and elsewhere. He lives in Lawrence, Kansas.

Printed in the United States
by Baker & Taylor Publisher Services